THE GIRL
WITH THE
CRYSTAL EYES

THE GIRL
WITH THE
CRYSTAL EYES

BARBARA BARALDI

Published by

MAXCRIME

an imprint of John Blake Publishing Ltd,
3 Bramber Court, 2 Bramber Road,
London W14 9PB, England

www.johnblakepublishing.co.uk

First published in Italy by Mondadori as *La Bambola di Cristallo*, 2008
This edition 2010

ISBN: 978 1 84454 930 6

British Library Cataloguing-in-Publication Data:
A catalogue record for this book is available from the British Library.

Design by www.envydesign.co.uk

Printed in Great Britain by CPI Bookmarque, Croydon CRO 4TD

1 3 5 7 9 10 8 6 4 2

Translated from the Italian by Judith Forshaw

Papers used by John Blake Publishing are natural, recyclable products made
from wood grown in sustainable forests. The manufacturing processes
conform to the environmental regulations of the country of origin

MAXCRIME series commissioning editor: Maxim Jakubowski

PROLOGUE

The fingers in the black satin gloves drum on the square table, filling the room with a muffled tune that fades into the emptiness that surrounds her. And she waits.

She sits with her legs crossed, lips red as desire itself, her blue eyes framed by lashes like a spider's web.

She glances at the large mirror with its inlaid frame, while with her other hand she plays with the golden curls falling in front of her face. The sofa is velvet, the carpet the colour of burnt earth. Finally, her eyes come to rest on the open petals of the roses in the Chinese porcelain vase, the centrepiece of the table.

They give off their perfume so generously – wanting nothing in return for the beauty they provide our senses with, she thinks.

A petal detaches itself and falls onto the shiny wooden surface of the table just as he appears in the doorway.

The tapping of her fingers suddenly stops. All that remains is silence, the silence of their exchanged gaze.

1

The man is wearing a dark grey suit, cut very loosely. The fabric seems to hiss as he walks towards the girl, his eyes fixed on her with the hint of a smile on his lips. He stops and puts a sweaty hand on her white thigh.

There is a ring on his finger, a symbol of some oath he no longer remembers, or that he has buried deep within his memory.

Now his smile widens, revealing teeth yellowed by sin. He can already taste the sweetness of a fruit that has been out of his reach till now.

Arousal makes him breathe heavily. His eyes, small and dark, run up and down her body, leaving behind the slimy trail of his thoughts.

'You've got no knickers on – like I asked you?'

'Of course. I'm a very obedient girl.' Languidly, she gets up and then sits down again on the table, leaning with her back almost up against the perfumed flowers. 'I adore roses. Because they've got thorns.'

'Go on, prick me. Then I'll punish you like you deserve.' And he falls on her.

Her quick, small fingers pick up a rose. But it's not the rose's thorns that pierce the man's flesh but a kitchen knife, sharp and shining, that enters deep into his chest and then slides out again, spurting hot, dark, dense drops of blood that splash the perfect features of her face.

In and out, in and out. The blade is like a silver fish jumping in and out of the waves at dusk, leaving the viewer's gaze adrift in the water, like a thought without an end.

The end.

The blade drives in again and again, stabbing at the hands with which he tries to protect himself – in vain – then at his neck as he sinks on to the carpet, which is now the colour of death.

The roses strewn over the table bathe their delicate petals in the blood that now covers everything. The blood soon fills the room with a cloying, suffocating fragrance.

The porcelain doll wipes her face with her black gloves. She tries not to slip on the sticky pool under her feet, while she leans over and starts to go through the man's pockets. He seems to be looking at her, his face distorted by a grimace of agony.

Here's the envelope. She opens it impatiently, then smiles.

'You were obedient, too,' she says, before turning her back on him and leaving.

She takes a last look in the gilded mirror, a mirror that wouldn't be out of place in a fairytale – a fairytale that's frightening but where she's the fairest of them all. Beautiful just as she is, smelling of blood.

CHAPTER 1

'What did you get up to last night?' Viola asks, without looking at him.

He doesn't answer her, as he carries on cutting his rare steak.

'What'd you do last night?' She glances at him fleetingly. Her blue eyes appear black because of her anger, because of the doubt that has taken root inside her.

'You're so insecure. I can't stand insecure people, you know?' He pushes back his hair without putting down his fork. The fork smells of blood.

'You're what makes me insecure. I wasn't like this before I met you,' she lies.

Viola is beautiful and has a good figure, and she always smells nice – naturally. She has good skin. 'I'll ask you one last time, and then I'm going.' And she stresses every word, as if she's reciting some magic spell that will open a secret door behind which is hidden priceless buried treasure. 'What did you do last night?'

He stops chewing his steak and raises his eyes from his plate to look at her. She has big breasts, squeezed into that stretchy top that she got from the 'everything two Euros' stall in the market. He still fancies her, he decides, and he'd happily fuck her right now if he could. He swallows his mouthful of steak. 'I was at Luca's, watching the match. We had a few beers and then fell asleep on the sofa, you know.' He puts a big chunk of meat in his mouth and smiles. 'That's all, baby. That's all.'

She feels able to breathe again, but her words stick in her throat, fixed there by fear.

'I don't like it when you do that,' is all she manages to say. And she covers her face to hide two single tears, the tears she never manages to hold back when they argue.

They're always the same tears; she realises that. The same tears that appear without fail every time they have a fight. Right from the first time they'd argued, the day of their first date outside the Quadrifoglio Pizzeria, when his hands seemed to be everywhere at once and she had had to stop him.

'Gently,' she had murmured.

In a fit of rage, he had exploded suddenly, like a firecracker too full of powder, leaving her terrified. In the end, she had burst into tears, and only then had he calmed down and had hugged her, making a vague and clumsy show of kindness.

Marco was a truly average man. A man with clichés in his veins instead of blood.

'Would you like anything else?' asks the waiter. He has been keeping an eye on them, waiting for them to calm down, not wanting to risk losing the usually generous tip that Marco leaves when he's in good company and also in a good mood.

'Yes, a coffee. A coffee with Sambuca,' he replies. When Marco says certain words – like coffee – there's still a trace of his southern accent.

The waiter looks to Viola. She's the most beautiful of the girls he's seen with The Thug. They call him that in this restaurant because of what he looks like, but also because of the way he speaks, a bit aggressive and never showing any respect.

'Nothing for me, thanks,' she answers politely.

Marco leaves his usual tip, and winks at the waiter. That wink means he's going to sleep with the girl he's now with.

'I've scored again, Giacomì,' he always says, slapping the waiter on the back as he gets up from the table, eyeing up the arse of whichever girl he's with this time, while she heads towards the door.

CHAPTER 2

Eva gazes at the small white daisy, its petals edged with pink, which keeps her company, sitting on the overcrowded desk, a constant reminder of an overwhelming workload.

She doesn't know it yet but, while she sits there, every day a little piece of her dream deserts her, a dream she's had since she was only small. She tells herself that tomorrow will be different, that it won't always be like this, that soon they'll take her ideas seriously and she'll have her big chance. To help herself believe it, every now and then she lets her mind drift away as she contemplates the fresh flowers placed on duty on her desk, adding colour to that grey corner of the office, and she loses herself in daydreams as intangible as the smell of snow.

When she was a kid she adored adverts – she loved them almost more than cartoons. She liked the characters in adverts: the chicken Calimero because he was shy and clumsy, Coccolino the teddy bear because he was gentle and could talk, and she even thought the freckly kid who ate milk chocolate was really nice. On the other hand, bad adverts got on her nerves. What point was there in talking about quality or savings while walking round a supermarket in a bathrobe, or stuffing yourself from a plate piled high with snacks before you went to work?

So she'd always known what job she wanted to do when she grew up. After a quick degree in communications, here she is bent over a desk at Art&Work, an advertising agency in Bologna. Always arriving at least ten minutes early every morning, with a ready smile and a great deal of imagination. Gradually, as time went on, she saw that she always ended up doing the same lowly, unskilled job and, instead of getting closer, her dreams drifted further and further away. As in an advert, she saw her dreams fly higher, while she, tiny as an ant, jumped up and stretched out her arms but never managed to grab hold of them.

Eva does the cut-outs of photographs. Eva researches products. Eva photocopies at the speed of light. Eva is a wizard with the scanner and saves mountains of images on autopilot.

'Roberto, excuse me, can I say something?' she had once said to the creative director, overcoming her shyness. The creative director was someone who turned up every morning preceded by a fake smile, his fedora worn at an angle, and sporting one of his op-art ties that made your eyes hurt.

'Of course you can.'

'Sorry, but I couldn't help noticing the sketch you've done for that prunes advert, and…' She paused for a moment.

'And?'

Pluck up the courage and tell him, she thought to herself.

'It's brown.'

'It's brown?'

'Yes, it's brown.'

'And what's the problem?'

'Brown, prunes, laxatives.'

'Eva…' A pause for him to gather his words and fire them at her, like an action hero firing bullets from a machine-gun. 'Eva, first, it isn't brown; it's a khaki colour. Second, I've worked in advertising for years and I've been behind successful campaigns, and I think I can manage without your advice, don't you?' He stopped, his two raised fingers open in a giant 'v' that seemed ready to swallow her – or rather a huge victory sign about to crush her.

Roberto is fucking Mariangela.

Overtime means fucking Mariangela in every possible position.

Mariangela is married to a much older man, very rich, who presented her with the advertising agency to give her something to do outside the house – her lovers being an added extra with the package.

After having won and married her, everything changed for them. Sex, for example. 'Before you have a woman, you imagine how she makes love, how she moves when she's under you, what noises she makes when she comes. You're generous as a lover,' he liked to say – often – to his few friends, 'but then everything changes. Two fucks and you're like brother and sister.' For his sister, he had opened a shoe shop – he really was generous to his relatives, Mr Dicarmine.

The day the publicity campaign for the laxative prunes was to be presented to the client, Eva joined in the hearty congratulations paid to the great creative talent who had produced an advert of such good taste and originality. The sun-dried prunes, against a background of beautiful bright yellow, made you think of the Californian sun and conveyed the idea of wholesomeness, of a product good to eat.

'Eva, you'd like my job, wouldn't you? Tell me, what colour background would you have used to advertise these prunes?' Roberto had asked, just to humiliate her, certain that she wouldn't dare say a word. 'Perhaps a nice brown?' he had added, without giving her time to speak and provoking, unsurprisingly, a burst of laughter from everyone else.

Eva had clenched her fists and had then gone back to her scanning, and had lost herself in the potted violet sitting on her desk.

A violet far too perfumed to be condemned to die on that grey desk. Grey like her shattered dreams.

CHAPTER 3

I feel empty.
Empty like a night without him.

He has gone out again this evening. He splashed on some aftershave and smoothed gel into his hair, put on his light-coloured jeans and a tight white T-shirt. I hadn't even seen that T-shirt before. It must be new. He must have bought it without me, and he didn't even show it to me.

And me, I'm stuck here alone on the sofa, in my pyjamas.

I'm just a pair of pyjamas with a soul.

I'm feeling so, so tired. And I was twenty only a week ago.

She closes her eyes to lose herself in her memories, those memories of when she was small. Her father. The week of her birthday. Seven days full of music and surprises. Yes, there was always music in the background.

It was the rule.

'Birthdays are the personal celebrations we all have.

Which means they're the most important. Do you follow me, Viola?'

'Yes.'

'Listen to me carefully. Everyone celebrates Christmas, and at Easter every child gets their chocolate egg, the ones with a surprise inside…'

'Yes.' She was then hardly more than a metre tall.

'But a birthday, that's just yours, *your* day, the day when you're a princess and we all have to pay lots of attention to you.' And he would bow to her.

She used to laugh and gaze up at him.

'One day isn't long enough to celebrate such an important event; we need at least seven days…' That was the rule. Seven days, not a single one less.

Her father used to listen to the records of Franco Battiato.

Perhaps it's because of this indulgence that she doesn't have a permanent centre of gravity, and she's always changing her opinion about things and about people. How happy she was when her father was there, the man in her life.

She cries.

She often cries, perhaps every day, at least for a minute. She's never understood why she cries so much.

Too much.

Today she has cried twice. The first time when she woke up, after having made love with him, and she found a love bite on Marco's neck – it turned out to be a bruise.

'A bruise,' she says out loud.

And the second time – now – while she listens to Battiato on her own, seated on the sofa in her pyjamas.

I'm alone and I turned twenty less than a week ago.

Twenty years to realise that perhaps Mr Right, the man every girl is waiting for, was there for me as soon as I was born, but with a sell-by date.

It lasted ten years. That's what was written on the box.

She cries.

Battiato's *Bandiera Bianca* – 'White Flag' – is playing in the background.

She falls asleep while the white flag flutters on the bridge.

She finds herself walking in the sun. Her shadow follows just a step behind her.

She is alone, with only her shadow for company. But then she turns and sees them: the cars speeding by alongside her. She feels a rush of air every time one passes her. She gets closer and closer to a metal rail, and she realises she's feeling slightly afraid.

She carries on walking. Now the cars are still, and there is silence. Suddenly there's no noise.

A closed door.

She stops and stares at it. She looks back for a moment, and realises that her shadow isn't there any more.

It's impossible. She turns round but she still can't see it. And yet the sun is still shining, right above her.

The door. All that's left now is the door. As if the world and all of life were suddenly there behind that door.

She opens it.

She is engulfed by speed, a sudden whirlwind of it,

wrapping around her. Blood. Blood everywhere. And those eyes.

Staring eyes that are fixed on her, peering out of the blood.

She gets up suddenly, breathing heavily; on the bridge the white flag has stopped flying. Inside her, everything is red.

A red river. She is trembling, unable to stop it.

She picks up her mobile phone, with its worn cover and the Powerpuff Girls flying above the sky-blue skyscrapers, and she calls him.

He doesn't answer.

'The number you have called is…'

She doesn't want to know for sure that he might have switched his mobile off.

She gets to her feet, opens the fridge and takes out the milk. Milk and chocolate. Milk, the drug of choice for babies. A drug that calms you down, that tastes of pleasant dreams. She drinks her milk and turns off the light.

She stretches out on the sofa – a sad pair of pyjamas. A pair of pyjamas with a soul.

CHAPTER 4

Miew looks out of the window. The reddish evening light washes over everything; it shrouds the city, transforming it and distorting every harmony, while she waits for her owner to return.

Soon she will hear the sound of her footsteps running up the stairs, heavy because of the combat boots she always wears, jumping two steps at a time to get home quicker, the key in the lock and her voice, soft but slightly shrill, saying: 'Come on, don't be in a huff. I had to work late today.'

She looks out. The red is becoming black, and it's as if the city is changing its clothes. Now it is becoming mysterious, but also cruel, like a devastatingly beautiful woman who plays with the affections of a dejected lover.

Via San Felice, narrow and smelling of piss.

A puddle of dried vomit from last weekend, which now seems a long time ago. Graffiti on the wall, shouting a message that no one understands. A cat yawning.

Eva walks quickly, clenching her fists. She glances into the Irish pub. She often used to go there when she was younger.

An old child, that's what she feels like – an old child.

A child who doesn't know anything, yet knows everything about life.

Disillusion – it's a good word, but it hurts. It hurts her deep in her heart.

It's dark now. She had to work late.

She walks quickly, feeling the air on her face. It's cold.

Eva has never had a boyfriend.

She used to try to picture what her first boyfriend would be like, but she was never able to come up with a complete image. There was that game, *Gira la moda*, when she was a girl, in the Eighties. There was a wheel and you spun it round; you filled in the type of hair you'd like, then the face, the breasts, the legs, and finally the shoes.

She used to create fabulous girls, but the game never worked when she tried to create in her head the ideal boy – someone you'd lose your head over.

And, perhaps out of spite, he had never appeared in real life either.

Fear, lack of interest, who knows.

She has never had a boyfriend. Never kissed a boy.

She was curious, at school, listening to what her friends said. 'He kisses well. His lips are nice – soft and full.' 'Luca's got a huge package. Last night I gave him a blow job.'

Art lessons were when they shared their secrets.

'But do you lick him, or just move your mouth up

17

and down?' It was as if they were writing a guide to the perfect blow job.

But she hadn't even understood properly how you did it, a blow job. The half phrases she overheard did more harm than good.

The result: it made her sick to her stomach to think about having to lick and suck that 'thing', a thing that then spat out some sort of sour-tasting stuff. But the stories about how it was like gagging on chewing gum always drew a crowd.

By the end of her fifth year, and after all those sessions in the art room, she had realised that giving blow jobs was too dangerous a skill, requiring too much practice for a girl like her.

She walks quickly.

She thinks about Miew.

CHAPTER 5

Absent-mindedly, Marconi passes through the waiting room and notices yet again the girl with red hair and blue eyes – such a pale, piercing blue.

He's sure he has seen her at least twice already in the last few days.

He wants to ask her if she needs any help, but Tommasi calls him over to talk about that case of the boy without a residence permit, who they'd arrested the week before during an attempted robbery in a bar in Strada Maggiore.

'I'm coming,' he mutters to himself, while he gives her a last look.

She drags her gaze away from the window and looks at him for a moment.

She reminds him a lot of his first girlfriend, who was beautiful but always sad. At school she'd kept to herself, perhaps because of her hair, or possibly because of the freckles sprinkled across her oval face. He had never understood why she was sad, nor did that matter to him. It didn't matter because he liked her, and one day he had waited for her and, instead of running home with the other boys, he had walked with her as far as the police barracks.

Even just talking about her father struck fear into him. The man was a warrant officer.

An officer. Just a single word that spoke volumes to him.

They hadn't spoken at all on the way home, then, looking at his feet, he had asked her: 'Do you want to be my girlfriend?'

'Yes.'

Just the one word, accompanied by a smile.

The next day neither of them approached the other because they were too shy, and the great love of their fourth form ended before it began. At the end of the school year she moved with her parents to Milan, and he had been left with a heaviness, a bad feeling, like a feeling of failure, a sense of emptiness.

'So, how are we doing?'

'We can't get out of it,' Tommasi replied. 'The Moroccan consulate says he's Tunisian. The Tunisian consulate says he's definitely Moroccan. It's always the same. Another guest for the detention centre.'

'By the way, what was up with Morini this morning?'

'I think his wife doesn't give him any. But have you seen her? Such a nice piece of skirt for such a –'

'OK, Tommasi, stop thinking about Morini's wife. They found the documents of that woman who came in last week, the one who had her bag snatched at the market. She hasn't answered the phone for two days, so get the car keys and we'll go and check that everything's OK with her.'

Tommasi isn't very tall. He has black eyebrows that meet in the middle, a fleshy mouth, small ears.

He picks up the identity card. 'What do you expect? She's eighty, so she's probably a bit hard of hearing.'

'Well, it means that we'll be doing a good deed, doesn't it? Every now and then it doesn't do any harm.'

'Of course, Inspector.'

In the waiting room, the seat by the window is now empty. For a moment Marconi thinks she was just a dream.

CHAPTER 6

*B*ut do you love me?
Marco is in front of the mirror, looking at himself, his chest damp from the aftershave just applied. He has a bit of a belly – the result of a few too many beers – but she finds it sexy.

But do you love me with just a tiny bit of the sort of love you see in films? Viola looks down.

He closes the bottle of aftershave that smells of musk and picks up his comb. He runs it through his thick black hair, which is still wet. He watches his reflection in the mirror. The mirror image of himself. He loves himself.

Do you love me at least a bit, even just a small amount compared with how much I love you? Yes, because I love you. I love you, and unlike all those who say they don't know what love means, I do know. I know what it means to love someone.

I know that it means doing things even if you don't want to, even if they're not really you. Just because the person you love likes them.

I know that it makes you breathless.

Air. There's no air when you're not here, and I'm always afraid that you won't come back to me and then I start crying. I cry if I think that you'll leave me one day, and clearly this means that I love you, and then when I hear your voice I tremble a bit and then... And then I wish you wouldn't go out again tonight, but if you really want to I'll hardly say a word – just the mildest objection – and then I'll let you do what you want, as always.

Because I love you.

And you, do you love me?

He turns and grabs the white shirt that he's left in the bathroom. He slips it on with an expansive movement of his arms; for an instant he looks like he's swimming.

He fastens the bottom button, then the next two up. He leaves the rest undone. His chest is waxed, smooth as an eel. He never takes his eyes from the mirror as he gets ready.

When he's finished, he raises his eyebrows and gives a smile that Viola can clearly see. It's a ghost of a smile but it says so much, not least that he's going out again tonight.

He turns suddenly and heads towards the semi-darkness of the corridor. 'But what the fuck are you doing there, in the dark? God, you nearly gave me a heart attack.'

'I was coming to call you. There's a good film about to start.'

'What are you on about? I'm going out, I told you.'

'But...'

'No buts, sweetie.'

23

CHAPTER 7

The chopping board sits on the work surface between the fridge and the sink. She remembers that it has always been there. There is the table linen with the blue cockerel and the crocheted edge, the piece of decorative ironwork – a local tradition – hanging on the wall, and next to it a small image of Saint Anthony, the patron saint of animals.

It's a kitchen typical of the Romagna region, like the Sangiovese wine made from grapes grown by Marietto, the farmer who lives at the end of the road – where they've now widened Via San Vitale. Marietto, brandishing his hoe, is always swearing at the cars as they go past, and at politicians, and at the government.

At the dining table, the questions are always the same. 'You *are* eating properly, aren't you?' asks her mother. 'You look thinner.'

'Have you met any trendy people yet? Do you go out a lot in the evening?' asks her thirteen-year-old sister, apparently without needing to pause for breath.

Eva has learned to lie, and is very good at it, keeping her answers vague so that there's no risk of forgetting the details.

'Yes, I've met lots of nice people. There's one girl I go and see a film with every Tuesday evening. And they've finally given me more responsibility at work – I'm helping out on an advertising campaign they're creating soon for a new shopping centre in San Lazzaro.'

The television is on, providing the background noise to their chatting.

Time passes between the pasta (lasagne or cappelletti), the roast chicken or cold cuts and bread, and finally the coffee. Then it's time for a quick game of cards while they digest their meal and each of them gets a chance to show off. They play in pairs, the two sisters against their parents. They exchange coded looks and signals to distract their opponents and mislead them. The old trick of looking unhappy when you have a good hand almost always works. The first to get to seven is the winner, no objections allowed. When her father loses he gets angry, and sometimes some colourful phrases in local dialect slip out. He gets up and goes into his study to get himself a shot of grappa.

'Bye. I'll be back on Sunday evening.' Eva strokes Ken, the guard dog, or rather the dog that used to be their guard dog. He's got seven scars – and a half – and his ear was almost ripped off by the neighbour's cat. It was definitely the cat, even if Paolino doesn't agree. He insists that Tibia couldn't have had anything to do with it, that his cat is well behaved.

Eva knows the way home by heart: for a year and a half she's been going backwards and forwards between Bologna and Ravenna, to spend the odd evening or a Sunday with her parents.

Before she began living with Miew, she used to sleep in her old room on Saturday nights, so she could spend the whole weekend with her family.

By the sea.

It's the sea that she misses most. The sea in winter, but in autumn as well, and in spring.

Not summer, though. She doesn't miss the sea in summer, because of the tourists. She never likes going down to the sea in the summer. It's too busy, with too many deckchairs.

How many Sunday mornings has she spent walking along the shoreline, even when it's raining or there's that wind that makes you feel restless – caressing your hair and making it stiff because of the salt, and then you've no choice but to wash it.

She used to wake up early, call her sister with the promise of a plate of fried fish and a glass of white wine at the canal port, and then she'd head down to the empty beach, the one between Ravenna and Punta Marina.

She would walk along, bending down to pick up shells. She looked particularly for those cone-shaped shells you hardly ever find in one piece, but when you do they bring good luck.

The sea makes her think about her life. But not too seriously – thoughts empty out of her head and she doesn't look too deeply inside herself.

Eva just lives, nothing more. She doesn't ever ask

herself whether she's actually happy. And after all, what is happiness?

Since she's had Miew, everything has changed. It was inevitable that she would lose something when such a special new friend arrived. When something really beautiful happens, you always need to establish a new balance. The proportion of good and bad always has to stay the same, Eva reckons. She has always thought that.

'God, I need to pee. I can't wait any longer,' she says aloud, interrupting the flow of her own thoughts. She slows down to look for a lay-by where she can stop.

I don't understand why they design them like this. It's gross.

She switches on her indicators even though there's not a soul around. She then gets out of the cocoon of her car.

Brrr, it's cold.

The steaming pee on the icy tarmac creates a little cloud of hissing fog. She likes to watch herself while she pees. She smiles.

The headlights of a car that seems to be slowing down. Two round eyes of white light shine on her as she hurries to shake off the last drop, so she can pull up her trousers. *Fuck. Someone would turn up right now. So much for privacy*, she thinks while she walks faster to get back in her car.

The yellow eyes go dark. Silence surrounds her. That silence that you only hear at night.

By day, silence is noisier.

She pulls the car door open, her thoughts already elsewhere, but then something stops her violently: a shadow by her side, a shadow that frightens her, the shadow of a short, thin man, with a moustache. He is staring at her.

With a look that she's never seen before.

Time stops for a moment; she doesn't move – or understand. She just feels an overwhelming terror that probes into her flesh and brings a lump to her throat.

He pushes her hard, making her fall back against the passenger seat, so the gear stick presses against her spine. He doesn't give her time to get up again. In a second he is on top of her, pinning down her hands, brushing her face with a moustache that smells of tobacco while he tells her to stay still or he'll hurt her.

She shouts, but makes no sound. She feels wetness because of the tears streaming down her face.

The man slaps her, making a noise that reverberates in the silence and surprises her.

'Shut up, bitch. Don't make a sound. Stop that!' he says angrily, his eyes wild, his mouth drooling. Then he lets go of her with his left hand so he can undo his trousers.

Obscene words are muttered through clenched teeth while he fondles her breasts, hurting her.

'No!'

'Shut up, bitch. I know you want it. You're all the same – you play hard to get but really you like it. Come on, take me in your mouth! Do it! Do what I tell you!'

He holds her down. He's astride her and he tries to put himself in her mouth, while she turns her face from side to side, one arm held down above her head.

He lets go of her again. Another slap. Nastier, harder, this time.

A moment's pause.

To die.

Or to live.

She's like a wounded deer. She reaches for the rock she keeps in the tray at the bottom of the gear stick. It's blue, smooth and shiny, in the shape of an egg. It is her good luck charm, a souvenir from a trip to Sardinia with her family.

She clutches it tight. It's like an artificial hand, an extension made of hard stone. She lifts it up, strikes him.

Just one blow, and he falls backwards. He slumps against the car door, his mouth hanging half open.

His prick, still hard, looks up at her, surprised.

His body slides down into a puddle.

Eva watches him fall and doesn't move.

The good luck charm is in her hand. It's still her hand, but now it's covered in blood.

CHAPTER 8

'Why don't you open it?'
   'What is it?'
'Just open it!'
'But why are you giving me a present? Is there something you've done that I have to forgive you for?'
'You complain that I don't pay you enough attention, and then when I buy you a present it's because I've got something to hide. You're never happy, Viola. What am I to do with you?' And he turns away from her.
She gets up. She's now wearing an apricot-coloured jersey dress.
'I'm sorry, sweetie.' She takes his hand. 'I'll open it straight away.'
She tries untying the shiny bow, but can't undo it. She pulls at it some more. The skin on her fingers turns white, as if the blood has stopped flowing.
'Use the scissors,' Marco has already run out of patience.

'They're somewhere in the kitchen, and I want to open it straight away.'

He takes the present, ripping off the bow, and lets it fall to the floor.

She claps her hands and jumps about in her seat.

'That's it – tear it off. It'll bring me good luck!'

A white box. She opens it.

A black, see-through slip.

Marco buys her very few presents. But when he does, it's always lingerie.

'Try it on for me.'

'Now?'

'Yes, do it for your lover.' His eyes shine with desire.

'OK.'

Viola puts the white box on the table and holds up the slip.

'It's beautiful.'

She turns to go into the bedroom, to put it on.

'No, here. In front of me.'

'I don't like changing here. I'll go into the bedroom and I'll be back straight away.'

'Come on, what are you embarrassed about? What's the difference? I know what you look like.'

'No, I'd be embarrassed. I'd feel strange.'

He grabs her wrist. 'For me,' he says to her, with a smile on her lips.

Viola has always had a boyfriend. Ever since she was thirteen, perhaps to fill the gap left by her father. Perhaps because she really isn't someone who can live on her own.

And she's never able to say no.

'OK.'

31

She takes off the dress. It keeps the shape of her body as it lies on the sofa.

She's wearing a white vest, which matches her panties. Her bra is black, though, one of those minimiser bras.

He's sitting on the chair opposite her.

Viola hesitates for a moment.

He signals to her with a nod, barely raising his head. Like a silent command. A command she can't question.

She slides down one strap, then the other. The vest falls to the ground.

'Everything,' he says.

The panties... and the bra last. She takes it off slowly.

Her breasts are soft but firm.

She immediately covers herself with her arm.

As she puts on the slip, he stands up.

CHAPTER 9

Miew looks at her from the threadbare armchair in the corner of the room.

She looks like she's dead, covered completely by the yellow bedspread that crushes her like a heavy gravestone.

Eva isn't dead. But she wishes she were.

She wishes she could press the off switch of her life; then peace and silence.

Cancel everything. Delete the images that appear in front of her eyes and never go away.

But there is no peace. There is no forgetting.

She is curled up amid that dull pain, the pain of someone who has lost everything in an instant.

Faith. Losing one's faith means being dead. Dead inside.

The sun flows in through the cracks in the darkness, creating thin lines of light.

The phone rings insistently. At the other end is Sonia, who doesn't understand why Eva's late, and is worrying about the package of images waiting to be scanned that's leaning against her empty desk.

There's a wilting flower on that desk as well.

Eva, lost in a bed that smells of tears, thinks about an advert she really liked when she was a girl. An advert for those biscuits with a hole in the middle of them. It featured a sad little girl, who was alone. Then she slipped a biscuit on her finger, as if it were a ring, and, as if by magic, everything became beautiful. A happy jingle started playing, and a white unicorn appeared. She climbed on to its back and together they flew away.

Miew jumps up on the bed.

The small black cat starts to rub herself against the girl's hair, her purring so low that it's almost imperceptible. Perhaps Miew wishes she could turn into that same winged horse, the horse in the biscuit ad, and carry Eva far away.

The telephone rings.

Miew miaows more loudly. She touches Eva's arm with her paw. Little prods, just to rouse her, to get her attention.

Eva gets up slowly. She drags herself into the kitchen and automatically pours the cat food into the bowl with stars on it.

MIEW is written on the bowl. It's a present she gave her cat to celebrate their first year together.

The little cat rubs herself backwards and forwards against Eva's legs. Every now and then she stops and looks up, searching for Eva's gaze.

She doesn't find it. Her mistress's eyes are empty; there's no light in them any more. Just shadow.

They're different. Perhaps they'll never be the same again.

CHAPTER 10

The sun is high in the sky. It must be about midday. It doesn't feel hot, but the unforgiving sun smothers everything with a bright, yellow light. Her shadow follows a step behind her as she walks, alone, in the sunlight. Cars rush by next to her. She can feel their speed as vicious splinters of air that stab at her legs and make her begin to lose her balance.

She starts to run. She's afraid. She runs, and every so often she looks back to check on her shadow. It's still there, following her, black and straight. Her shadow.

She reaches a wide open space, an expanse of grey cement stretching into the distance. Silence, nothing but a deafening silence. And a door. Closed. In front of her.

She stands still and stares at it, then starts to feel anxious. No, it can't have happened again. She turns suddenly to look at the shadow. Her shadow.

It has vanished.

She looks up at the sky. The sun is still there, shining down on that flat surface, a sea of tarmac.

All that's left now is that closed door. The end of the world. A closed door.

She stretches out her hand, but she doesn't open the door straight away. First, she turns round one last time. Her shadow isn't there; it has been swallowed up by all that grey, the grey expanse that now appears to be overheating under the pitiless sun.

She hurries to open the door.

Everything starts to spin fast. And then faster.

Blood everywhere, and those eyes. Wide-open eyes that stare at her, out of the blood.

She screams and finds herself back in her crumpled bed, dripping with sweat and clutching the edge of the blanket. Her teddy bear is on the floor; he looks at her with fear in his eyes. The sun caresses her through the sheer white curtains.

Her visions have started again. Oppressive. Devastating.

She wipes away the sweat with the palm of her hand, while with her other arm she reaches down and places the teddy bear back on her chest.

The terror she feels now blurs into the terror of her dreams.

The terror she felt when she saw it. Death, a cruel experience.

She was ten – it had been her birthday less than a week before.

So it was still her special week. And she had that same dream every night.

Darkness; a wet street.

The black car that sped over the tarmac.

A brightly coloured parcel on the back seat that slid from right to left as the car went round the corners.

The sound of brakes. A red river.

She's shaking; she isn't able to stop herself. She couldn't stop herself then, either.

She knows what it means for her to have dreams like this. The door has opened again.

The door. That's what her psychiatrist, Anna, called it when she was a child.

There are lots of doors inside our minds, she said. Some stay closed forever. Others open all of a sudden, letting us see fragments of things. Fragments of things that are about to happen. Or images from the past.

The door used to open as soon as sleep rendered her unconscious, vulnerable, fragile.

She used to find herself inside a crystal ball, but she wasn't able to see her future in it. She would get on her silvery horse, a brutal stallion that carried her to desolate lands. Ill omens. Death.

'Don't cry. Your dad loved you,' the man in uniform had told her.

'Look, he bought you this.'

The teddy bear. The same one she now clutches tightly.

CHAPTER 11

The arcade.

Eight o'clock at night.

Four boys smoking on the metal steps.

Around them, a glimpse of the world, shadows passing by, waiters inviting people into bars that are too brightly lit for eyes that are now accustomed to the dark street.

A man approaches. He is tall, well built.

'You're late.'

He doesn't answer.

'Have you got it?'

'Yes.'

Money is exchanged, and the small packet disappears quickly into the young man's pocket. He is wearing a green baseball cap, back to front.

The man doesn't even say goodbye; he goes back where he came from.

He leaves the darkness of the arcade, heading for the lights of Via Indipendenza.

Hands in his pockets, collar turned up.

He walks quickly, following the street ahead. If anyone comes towards him, they have to get out of his way. He doesn't move aside for anyone. He carries on in a straight line.

Every now and then he passes a girl in a short skirt, and slows down.

A whistle. A compliment of sorts that escapes through clenched teeth.

He stops in front of the window of a shop selling underwear. There are girls intent on choosing something to transform themselves for their Friday-night lovers. Because on Friday night all women become single. They tart themselves up, get their hair done, and go out with their friends. All of them smelling of perfume and dressed up in their finery. A glimpse of underwear and a fixed smile – just as he likes them.

He goes inside to get a better look at the merchandise. He wants to be a part of this celebration of vanity.

A young girl gazes entranced at a see-through thong.

'It'd look good on you,' he says. The girl looks at him out of the corner of her eye, and the watchful sales assistant comes towards him.

'Can I help you?' she asks.

'I was looking for something sexy for my girlfriend,' as he looks at the arse of a middle-aged woman, wearing a miniskirt and a short fur coat. *Not bad for her age, I'd give her one*, and meanwhile he lets the gauze of a pair of panties slide through his fingers.

CHAPTER 12

The red convertible speeds along the motorway, caressed by the sun.

The golden curls, tousled by the air rushing past, get entangled as they play with the wind.

The porcelain doll, her crystal eyes protected by big black sunglasses, like a diva from the 1930s, accelerates impetuously.

She's wearing leather gloves.

She loves the feel of leather against the steering wheel. She's sure it improves her grip, making her at one with the car, an Amazon in a black miniskirt and stockings.

A few drivers sound their horns as she passes; one sticks out his tongue and shouts words that would be bleeped on TV.

She doesn't hear them, doesn't see them.

She overtakes a fat man driving an electric blue lorry covered in lights. In the cab there's a sign that says *I'm your father* in English. Either side of this sign are two pin-ups with their tits out.

She speeds past him and then turns right, attracted by the sign of a motorway café.

'A coffee,' she orders as she sits down at the bar.

She drinks her coffee – boiling hot, no sugar – and she plays with her curls, wind-swept from the speed of the car.

Just at that moment, the fat lorry driver comes in. He sits down next to her.

'What's a beautiful girl like you doing all alone? Don't you want some company? Well, here's your daddy.'

She doesn't answer. Instead, she throws down a coin on the sea-green counter, and asks the pale girl behind it where the toilet is.

'Outside, at the back. But I wouldn't, if I was you. You know how it is... the customers here. Well, it's not very clean,' she adds, slightly embarrassed.

'That's OK.' She turns without waiting for her change.

She walks away. The lorry driver swears, then reveals his opinion of her in a drawl.

She goes into the washroom and admires herself in the mirror. She's beautiful, and she knows it. Then she turns her back on her reflection and pauses in front of the thin wooden door, marked with the silhouette of a figure in a skirt.

She goes in and shuts the door; then, without taking off her gloves, she lets her black lace panties slide down, careful not to let them touch the floor. She takes them off and holds them in her teeth, between red lips, while she balances on the toilet seat. And then she hears him come in.

'I smell a stuck-up little cunt,' the fat man says, sniffing.

41

She gets off the loo, puts her panties back on and straightens her miniskirt. Then she turns the key and opens the door.

He's standing in front of her. Looming.

He tells her he's not going to let her out, takes one step towards her, then another.

The doll moves backwards. Now he's inside the cubicle with her, and he closes the door behind him.

She smiles and lifts up her skirt. He smiles, too.

She removes her magic wand from the top of her hold-up stockings and caresses his throat.

He hasn't time to scream.

The artery in his neck has been sliced open with a small bronze razor that looks like a prop from some old film.

The blood sprays everywhere, staining the filthy walls.

It covers her.

It colours her.

His body collapses on to the ground and the blood keeps pumping out.

Beauty and the Beast, that's what you could call the scene. With everything a single colour: scarlet.

She goes back to the mirror and looks at herself to see if she has changed.

Yes, she's more beautiful when splashed with blood, but she washes away the scarlet marks on her face, dries herself with a paper towel, and leaves the washroom.

'Mummy, I want that teddy bear, I want it!'

'Stop it, Sofia. I told you: just a coffee for daddy – he's tired – then we're going.'

'No, I want the teddy. I want it, I *want* it!'

'Quiet. Look, it's such an ugly teddy – who knows how long it's been there, gathering dust.'

'But I want it!'

'OK, but stop that now. You go and get it, and then let's go to the toilet.' And she drags the child along by the arm, now doing what her mother tells her to without complaint.

'Don't sit down when you wee. And wash your hands straight after, Sofia.'

The child opens the door.

Her scream pierces through the blood-stained cubicle walls.

The teddy bear falls into the thick, brown puddle.

Its glassy eyes stare up at her, spattered with blood.

The short life of a tantrum.

CHAPTER 13

The doorbell rings but there's no sound from the flat beyond. The forgotten kingdom of a sleeping princess.

Bzzz.

I know you're there. Open the door.

Bzzz.

The princess gets out of bed. It's not the kiss of a prince that wakes her but the strident ringing, which is still calling her.

She can't even remember how long she's been hiding under the covers, trying to forget. Perhaps a hundred years have passed. Just like in the fairytale.

Bzzz.

'Who is it?'

'It's Giulia. I wanted to see how you are,' says the voice on the other side of the door.

'Not very well, Giulia.'

'But aren't you even going to let me in? After I've climbed those stairs. At least for a glass of water...'

Eva unlocks the door; she doesn't say anything more.

'Hi. I didn't want to disturb you. It's just that you've been off work for days, so I got them to give me your address, because I thought I'd come and see you,' says Giulia, still out of breath. 'Isn't there a lift here?'

'It's fake.'

'What do you mean, it's fake?'

'The shaft's there, but the door's always been closed. There isn't a lift inside, or at least I don't think there is. They always say they'll sort it out sometime.'

Normally Eva would be overjoyed to have a visitor, but not now. She wants to be left on her own, here in the dark. She's forced herself to phone work and say that she has a really serious virus, in a voice sounding from beyond the grave. She did the same with her parents, adding that it was highly contagious so there would be no risk of them paying her a visit. She thought that that might allow her a few days of emptiness – of not existing.

'But how are you? You look awful.'

'I'm ill. I told you – I've got the flu.'

Giulia stands and stares at her, noticing how her colleague's eyes are puffy, with dark rings around them.

'Listen, you might be able to fool the others, but not me. I know what's wrong with you.'

Eva holds her breath for a moment.

'It's depression. It happened to me when my first boyfriend left me for some bitch on his course. You have to do something, Eva. I spent months and months going to a psychiatrist to try to accept what had happened, but in the end I realised that I had to rebel, get back on my own two feet. So I joined a gym,

I changed my hair – I changed my whole look – and I shopped more. It makes you feel better, you know?'

Eva is taken aback. She can't think of anything to say.

'People who are depressed withdraw into themselves. They think they'll feel better that way, but they're wrong. Luckily for you, I'm here now, and I'll help you. Because we women have to stick together or else we'll get trampled on by men, understand?'

Giulia talks without pausing, gesticulating with her hands while she looks round. It's as if she's filling up great big bubbles of air, and the more worked-up she gets the bigger the bubbles.

'And you'll never guess what's been going on at work – it's outrageous,' she adds. 'As soon as you were off sick, Roberto took advantage of me straight away – giving me loads of scanning to do. Sonia's being hysterical and then, you know…' a pause so she doesn't die from lack of oxygen, 'I understood what it was all about. That bastard's just getting even with me because two weeks ago he asked me out and I said no. But it won't end there. Oh no, it won't end there. Now, you get back on your feet and come back to work, and then we'll show them, won't we?'

'Sorry, Giulia, but really –'

'No excuses. I know how you have to cope when things like this happen. Now I'm going to make you something to eat.'

The girl carries on talking even as she empties the sink of an accumulation of cups, barely touching them with her fingertips.

It's clear that tidying isn't something she's used to, but, it seems, the result justifies this small effort.

'So all you've been living on is coffee and tea? It's no good: how are you going to get better if you don't eat?'

There's nothing Eva can say. Giulia wants to save her – or rather, make sure she returns to work as soon as possible. But the real reason doesn't really matter, since Giulia always gets what she wants.

'Is there anything to eat? Maybe some soup?'

'Under there. In the last drawer.'

'It's the only thing I know how to make. My ex was a fan of soup. It's not rocket science. Boil the water and throw in a stock cube and a bit of pasta. Got any stock cubes?'

'In the fridge.'

'A man who'll only eat soup definitely has no balls. Soup is for spineless people, no doubt about that. A plate of pasta is for men with hair on their chests. But I don't know why, if someone's a real man, you have to say he's got hair on his chest. Personally, I can't stand hairy chests, they make me ill. I like men to wax their chests. While the soup's cooking, go and have a shower. You smell a bit, you know.

'And who's this?' She looks down at the pussy cat who has appeared in the doorway.

'My flatmate, Miew. Miew, this is Giulia.'

'Pleased to meet you, Miew.' Giulia has already stopped looking at the cat.

CHAPTER 14

'Inspector Marconi, we're received the results from forensics,' announces Tommasi, still out of breath.

'Well, go on. What are you waiting for? Tell me what they say.'

'A real mess. The washroom was filthy; prints on top of prints. Seems it was only cleaned once a day, in the morning. That poor woman with her six-year-old daughter found the body at about half-past two. So you can imagine...'

'How's the little girl? Who questioned her?'

'Frolli intended to, but there was nothing doing. The girl was still in shock. Not surprising, really. She even dropped a teddy bear her mother had just bought her – straight into all that blood.'

Marconi shrugs his shoulders. As a kid, he wouldn't have liked to lose his favourite toy soldier in a pool of blood – blood that had gushed out of the slashed throat of a fat lorry driver – but perhaps it isn't the same these days, as children today aren't like they used to be. They're spoiled, too spoiled altogether.

'When the guys from forensics arrived, the body was still warm. They reckon no more than half an hour to an hour had passed before the body was found.'

'Are we sure that the mother didn't see anything? Frolli tried to reconstruct –'

'But what could they have reconstructed? The mother just wanted to take her little girl home – which I can understand. I've got her address here if you want it, but I don't think talking to her again would do much good.'

'You're right. Anything else?'

'Something odd. Next to the victim there was the print of a stiletto heel in the blood.'

'What do you mean?'

'And then the woman working in the café described a very beautiful woman wearing a miniskirt and hold-up stockings, who the lorry driver tried to chat up at the counter before she paid up and left. But we can't pay too much attention to what she says, the poor thing. Her colleagues say she drinks a bit, has done ever since her husband left her.'

'OK, Tommasi, let me be the judge of that. Pass me her statement.'

'Here it is.' The young man read it out with the hint of a smile on his lips. '"A beautiful girl came in; she looked like one of those girls on television. A model, beautiful, classy. She was tall and thin, with a short skirt and stockings that looked like silk. She was wearing leather shoes with very high heels, even her shoes were beautiful..."' My God, listen to this bit.

'"She gave me a two-Euro tip, and asked me where the washroom was. Then she smiled at me and went out, leaving behind her the smell of an expensive perfume." Who is this, a goddess?'

'Well, if she is a goddess, she's certainly not the sort who goes round granting the wishes of us mortals. Forget about the statement, then. What else is there?'

'Here we are. The victim died instantaneously. A clean, seven-centimetre cut across the throat. No sign of a struggle.'

'It must have happened quietly,' Marconi thinks aloud.

'Luca Cagnotto, forty-five years old, always been a lorry driver – everyone knew him. He drove a blue Iveco with a semi-trailer. He liked to fuck women. He often used to have them in the cab with him. In short, he liked that sort of company, but on that particular day he was alone.'

'And how can we be sure of that?'

'He had a radio, CB, on which he used to call himself "your father". That day he was alone – it's been confirmed by "Eagle", a friend of his, a lorry driver like him. He heard him on the CB half an hour before.'

'I don't know why they choose such stupid names.'

'Divorced – and the motorway police gave him some points on his licence a year ago for speeding. No criminal record.'

'But, after it was reported, didn't they think to block the motorway at the major exits.'

'They said it was already too late. No one made a decision.'

'Fuck!'

'Inspector.' Morini comes into the office without knocking, and visibly blushing.

'What is it? Now is not a good time.'

'There's a girl who says she has to talk to you. She's been waiting over an hour. She says it's important.'

'I've not got time now. Get her to tell you what it's about.'

'I've already told her that you're very busy, but she's adamant she wants to speak to you in person. She says she'll wait as long as she has to, but –'

'But everyone here *needs* something. Let her wait. I've got other things to do right now.' And he dives back into the file.

'It seems highly unlikely to me that a woman wearing high heels could have killed a tall, bulky man in a service station loo, all on her own. Just one push and you'd knock her over – a woman in stilettos.'

'Stilettos?' says Tommasi.

'You heard me. What can you tell me about the murder weapon?'

'There was an old-fashioned razor lying by the body. Some sort of antique, sharpened with real skill. But, Inspector!' Tommasi's face lights up. 'Perhaps the girl was there with the killer. Perhaps she's a witness.'

'No, the washroom's too small to fit a large man, the girl *and* the killer in, so either the girl came in when he was already dead – maybe she got frightened and ran away – or else she killed him herself. Any CCTV?'

'Nope, they've not been working for months. It's an old place. Just a small bar, the loos with a single entrance for both men and women, and two petrol pumps ouside.'

'Call the motorway people and get them to give you the licence plates from that stretch of road. From the week before to the day after. Perhaps we'll find something interesting.'

Tommasi is about to leave, but the inspector calls him back. 'Actually, get the registration numbers for up to a month before. This murder must have been planned. A service station without CCTV and with virtually unisex loos? A highly sharpened pre-war piece as a murder weapon?'

'So who's going to look at all those licence plates? And what are we actually looking for?'

'Give them to Morini – he still owes us a favour. Tell him to examine them carefully: you have to use your own instinct with such things. We're looking for the same cars going past at *different* times of day. There are commuters, it's true, but usually they always go past at the same time. So, who knows? Just do something.'

Tommasi hesitates for a moment with the file in his hand.

'Go on, then,' says Marconi as he sits down. Then he gets up again and looks out through the doorway. 'And the girl?'

'She left a couple of minutes ago,' answers a voice from the end of the corridor.

So she waited as long as she had to, thinks Marconi. *Women don't know how to wait. I've always said that.*

CHAPTER 15

She has been waiting for him for hours.
She's in bed, the covers pulled up to her neck.

On the bedside table lies a magazine previewing next summer's fashions. Impractical balloon-like dresses worn with ballet flats in pastel colours. She hates flat shoes. They make you waddle. She prefers shoes with heels, even if she can't wear them because then she'd be taller than Marco – which wouldn't be good.

A man has to be taller than his girlfriend: it's an unwritten rule, but it's true and that's that. Everyone knows it, and she knows it too.

She has just one pair of high-heeled shoes. They're beautiful – black, patent leather. She tries them on sometimes when she's alone in the house. She thinks she looks really good in them. They make her look slimmer.

But anyway, she can't wear them because of that tacit, international rule, and so she then puts them back in the box and tries not to think about them

As it is, she is condemned to wear only 'indefinable' shoes. Shoes that don't fit into any category. Flat, with laces. Sad shoes. Shoes that have always existed, but have never been in fashion.

She remembers that she removed her bitten nail varnish that afternoon, but then she forgot to repaint them.

It seems like a good way of passing the time, so, while she's still in bed, with the covers pulled up, she does her nails.

The polish is transparent – you can just about see it shining when her nails catch the light – but she can't go without nail varnish. A protective film. Her nails aren't then exposed; they're safe underneath, behind the shiny veil that smells so nice as you brush it on. Like the smell of petrol. Intoxicating.

But, like most of her other security blankets, it gives only the appearance of protection. Her nails aren't really safe.

She is the problem.

Or rather, she's the problem whenever she has one of her moments. *Those* moments.

Then she devours her nails as if they're sweets. She picks them clean with her teeth, like you do to the flesh of a crab inside its hard shell.

She does it as if she's in a trance, methodically, her eyes staring vacantly. In those moments she works fast, almost as if she has to finish before the rational part of her brain realises what she's doing. At the end she just feels an immense burning sensation, and her hands are no longer presentable – with those short nails that look as if they've been hammered into her flayed red flesh.

She paints the varnish on with the brush, carefully and slowly. She stops and looks at the nails that she has now made more beautiful, wiggling her fingers.

She smiles.

She thinks about the fact that she's now got just the little fingers left to do, and then time, in its erratic way, will drag by slowly again.

Too slowly. Like at school, when the bell never rang. When the teacher never stopped talking and her bottom would be numb from sitting on that uncomfortable chair.

At least she's comfortable now, here in bed, but time drags by just the same. Some things in life never change. And time is one of them – it passes by at whatever speed it wants, flying by when you're enjoying yourself, and counting out every breath when you're bored.

The other changeless thing is 'indefinable' shoes. Shoes that are never fashionable but that have always existed.

CHAPTER 16

'We're going to my beautician at lunchtime today. My treat.'

'What?' replies Eva while she carries on mechanically scanning images of tiles on behalf of a ceramics company.

'You're falling apart. You look like an old woman. You look like my grandmother!' says Giulia, tactlessly.

'You've already made me come back to work early, when I still don't feel well – so what do you expect?'

'I've been to a psychiatrist. I know what you need to do in these situations.'

If what Giulia said was written down, the word 'I' would be regularly underlined twice, in red. 'You can have whatever you want: massage, manicure, sunbed – and dad's paying.'

The girl's hands slide over Eva's white skin. Until now, Eva has only seen massages on television – in soaps where the current hunk takes the place of the masseuse so he can languidly caress the beautiful heroine.

But in reality 'the hunk' is a short, dark Filipina. Eva reckons she's darker than Filipinas usually are, but then, to tell the truth, she doesn't really know many.

In fact, she doesn't know any, so who knows why she expected the masseuse to have a lighter skin. *Like Indian women? No, perhaps Indian women are dark, too. People from the Far East surely have lighter-coloured skin. But which countries make up the Far East?*

The woman's small hands are extremely strong. She alternates delicate movements with energetic pummelling, using an oil that smells of flowers and mingles with the perfume of the patchouli-scented candles beside the bed.

The room is bare, dimly lit by the candles, and the faint background music provides a gentle accompaniment to the sound of dripping wax. The melting wax forms itself into shapes – first a female figure, then a flower – then it loses its shape and becomes just drops of wax again.

Eva isn't sure if she is enjoying the massage or not. She feels strange, almost defiled.

Her body doesn't want to unwind under the touch of those expert hands; her muscles – protecting her secret – fight against it and hurt.

Soon she feels an overwhelming desire to cry; she holds it back, but with difficulty.

'Don't be so tense, relax. Your spine's all seized up,'

says the girl in perfect Italian. Her accent sounds like she is from Bologna.

Eva blushes. She has read that massage can sometimes release traumas. She imagines them like pats of butter, and she sees them gradually melt away. Under the surface lies her secret.

What if the girl's busy fingers can see into her soul?

And what if there's a link between the masseuse's fingers, Eva's brain and her spine? *No, I can't let this happen.* And she tightens up even more.

'When you start to relax it'll feel nice,' continues the girl in a soothing voice, like the gentle, ethereal notes of the music fading into the air.

Eva doesn't want to relax. She hopes that this torture, which is supposed to be pleasant, will end soon. She's totally on edge.

She breathes a sigh of relief only when she finds herself back in the white corridor, heading towards the exit.

Giulia is there waiting for her. She seems pretty revved up.

'Eva, that was great! I've had a French manicure. And she holds up her hands. 'Look.'

Her nails are covered with clear polish, with just a thin strip at the tip of each painted white.

'Oh, that's a French manicure?'

'Yes, it's so elegant, isn't it?' She doesn't even give Eva time to answer. 'I had a go on the sunbed as well. It's a new type, low pressure, background music, mosaic tiles, wood trim. Fabulous.'

It's already dark outside, and it's cold.

They're in a street that runs parallel to Via Irnerio, where you feel like you're not in the city centre any more. Grey, anonymous buildings. Dark windows, lowered shutters. A faded peace flag hangs from the window of an upper storey.

They arrive at the tiny Indian takeaway at the corner of Via Mascarella.

I'm hungry.

It seems like her soul is speaking to her.

Hungry. Hungry for love. Hungry for attention. A chemical hunger. A desire to fill the emptiness.

The emptiness in my soul.

Giulia goes up the steps, and they're inside.

'I'm not eating,' says Eva, then adds hurriedly, 'I'll just keep you company.'

It's like a little cubbyhole, a mouse's nest. A counter just a metre long. A miniature fridge full of non-alcoholic beers and cans of iced tea. On the walls, posters of enormous platefuls of Indian food, each with a caption to explain what it is. Two tables arranged in an L shape with stools and a rubbish bin. Everything close together.

Then there's the television set. A television suspended in the air, as if it's meditating.

The screen projects fast-moving images from some subspecies of Indian MTV. A girl in a sari is singing, dancing, and winking. This girl and a guy, with what he hopes is a smouldering gaze, jump around in a music video, playing out a love story. Naturally it's a tale of unrequited love, and, just as naturally, it has a happy ending.

Another video starts.

'I don't believe it! Look,' says Eva. 'It's an Indian Take That!' And she laughs, the first time she has laughed for ages.

There are four men behind the counter. Four little mice in their nest full of provisions.

Isn't four too many? thinks Eva. Then she orders potatoes with paneer and spices. They're the best, their potatoes, and they only cost three Euros fifty. A proper meal, anyway.

Giulia studies her nails.

They don't chat; they have little to say to each other unless Giulia's doing the talking. They've been working in the same office for two years now, but they've never before been out together.

Before it happened.

Eva doesn't want to now divide her life into 'before it happened' and 'after it happened'.

It isn't fair if it becomes the most important thing in my life. In my calendar.

BI and AI.

Before it. After it.

But it did change everything.

The potatoes are good. As they always are. At least they *haven't changed.*

Miew stares out of the window. The light outside is still bright; meaning it will be hours until her only friend will return. That's how the cat measures time. For her, time is measured by Eva's absence.

When Eva goes out in the morning, Miew's life is put on hold. It only starts again in the evening when Eva opens the door.

Gradually, the daylight changes in its intensity. The light is like the ticking of a clock.

It's strange how humdrum life can be as it flows past.

Sometimes it's as if you're going through life without really realising it's you that's living it, but then, in an instant, all of a sudden, everything changes.

Everything is now bathed in a blue light. Eva is walking quickly under the arches of the arcades. The arches steal your memories, they transform them, they stretch them in the same way they have stretched a straight line to make it into a dome. The domes of the arcades look skywards 'with their noses turned up': that's what her grandfather had said when she was little and they had taken a trip to Bologna.

She starts walking again, with her head down, hands in the pockets of her black fleece. She has her hood up too, but it lets her rebellious blonde curls escape.

She looks at the boots she always wears. They're a sort of heavy talisman, keeping her feet firmly on the ground, attached to the floor. Without them she would daydream far too much. She isn't a practical person. The teachers always told her that at school.

She feels better. She feels reborn.

The baby girl of a sad woman who passed on her unhappiness even as she gave birth, and because of that Eva finds it difficult to smile. But now she's aware of something new deep in her heart. It's as if she's entering the world afresh, conscious of being able to do anything, of having risked everything and started again.

She can now see her block of flats in the distance. As she runs across the road, she spots a group of children who are laughing and shouting. And then she realises she's afraid.

CHAPTER 17

'Has the pathologist been yet?'

'Yes, Inspector. He says the man died between four and five,' answers Tommasi, clearly shaken by the early-morning sight of a corpse with its head smashed in, the body then abandoned among the rubbish in the University district.

'Cause of death?'

'His skull was split open. He was hit with force, with a stick perhaps. No trace of the weapon.'

Inspector Marconi paces irritably backwards and forwards. He is thinking, hard.

He approaches the body and lifts the white sheet for a moment. He studies the corpse.

He always looks at the expressions on the faces of the dead. You can understand so much by looking at them. He's sure of that.

'Move the body, if they've finished taking the photos. Fuck, this place is full of students. Who got here first?'

'Two men from the flying squad. One of them is that short guy leaning on the railing.'

The inspector walks towards Officer Gutuso – 'the Moor', as his colleagues call him – who is still staring at the white sheet covering the body. Muddy, brown loafers stick out from under the sheet.

He's staring because he's never seen a real dead body before, and now he can't take his eyes off it.

'Did you notice anything strange this morning, when you arrived?' Marconi tries to make eye contact with the officer, who is still looking unflinchingly at the dead man's shoes.

Gutuso is wishing that he hadn't been on duty earlier that morning. He'd rather have been in bed, especially now that he's finally found himself a girlfriend. And he wishes he hadn't seen him, the dead man. He thinks perhaps he'll see that same image in his dreams now, every night.

Then he frowns and nods. 'To tell the truth, yes. Something strange by the side of the body – a lollipop.'

'A lollipop?' Marconi repeats, astonished.

'Yes, strawberry,' adds the policeman. 'Still new – in its wrapper, I mean. It was propped up by the body, and he seemed to be looking at it… I mean, obviously he couldn't really have been looking at it, since he was dead.'

'*Obviously*,' Marconi interrupts, slightly irritated. 'But how come no one saw or heard anything?' he adds, raising his voice. 'Who called you, anyway?'

'An anonymous phone call. A man. Could've been a traveller. Sometimes they sleep here. This is where they hang out,' said the other man from the flying squad.

'Tommasi, go and get all the info you can. Ring doorbells; ask everyone who lives around here if they heard anything. See if you can find one of these travellers. Promise them a beer, if you have to. Go on now. I'll expect you in my office in an hour.'

Tommasi's a good officer, the inspector thinks to himself. He does what he's told without asking too many questions, he's bright and he doesn't say much. Marconi likes people who don't say much.

He goes into a nearby café. It's a small room with just enough space to stand at the counter, and with one small table with two chairs by the window.

'An espresso.' He orders in a tone that's rather too authoritative, causing the waiter give him a surly look. As he drinks it, he thinks about the strawberry lollipop. It's months now since he last had a good fuck; he can barely remember what a woman looks like.

Last time was with that Sabrina, one of his sister's friends – the one who's a bit of a slag and who had always wanted him. That evening he had met her in front of the gym when he'd come off duty and was heading home and he had given her a lift. She hadn't stopped looking at him while he was driving, and every now and then he had glanced briefly at her shapely thighs, squeezed into those ugly American, tan tights that made her look like a peasant. Or, rather, like someone's aunt.

Then she had invited him in, and he'd followed her without really wanting to, almost without thinking.

She was there in front of him, getting undressed, while she told him that she had always liked him, and that thinking about him going round with a gun had always excited her.

He had done his duty as a man, but it was a by-the-numbers performance, the sort you try to forget as soon as possible.

The coffee is extremely bitter – the *barista* getting his revenge? Now he's drying up cups and humming along to a song by Lucio Dalla that's playing on the radio.

'Excuse me, when did you close yesterday evening?' Marconi puts a Euro down on the wooden counter.

'What's it to you?'

'It's because of the dead man,' says Marconi and indicates a vague point somewhere outside the door, where the dead man lies, covered by the white sheet.

'Ah, you're a cop, that's it.'

That's it. What does 'that's it' mean?

'Ten o'clock, as always. And I didn't see or hear anything.' He goes back to the cups, and to the song.

Marconi decides to walk back to the police station. He enjoys walking: it helps him to think as well as relaxing him. It's a way of taking a moment just for himself, without having to explain to anyone what he's doing. He'd never be able to think things through at his desk, because it would feel like he was wasting time. Inactivity drives him mad; he has to be moving all the time.

A half-open door attracts his attention. He stops for an instant and can just make out, in an ivy frame, a statue of a naked girl covering herself with a hand resting lightly on her breast. She gazes out into the silence that surrounds her.

Someone has imprisoned her beauty within the marble, as an image of eternal youth. Her features will never change; she will never fall in love with another man; she will never run off to lead her own life; she will stay there.

Forever.

CHAPTER 18

Viola lets the water run over her. She plays with the scalding hot jet of the shower.

The rivulets of water follow the soft curves of her body.

She has taken the shower head from the wall, and now directs the jet of water to massage her body. The soles of her feet, then her hips, between her legs. Her delicate skin looks red. She likes it like that. She likes things that hurt a bit.

The same goes for when she makes love with Marco.

He is an animal. Not much foreplay – often he enters her straight away. He doesn't wait for her to get aroused.

And it hurts.

It hurts a bit – the way she likes it.

They argued again today. He went out and said he wouldn't be back for dinner and that she shouldn't wait up for him.

She cried first, and now she's burning herself with a scalding shower.

She wishes she didn't have to depart the white cloud of steam that surrounds her and protects her.

She decides to try out her water mantra.

Water – wash everything away. Wash it away and don't let me think. Make me new, without any worries, so I can be born again and be a princess.

It used to work when she was a girl, her magic water spell, but not now. Water never washes the hurt away. The hurt is too dark and too intense.

The dream has stopped persecuting her.

But this is when she feels even more frightened.

She steps out of the crystal box of the shower, resting her dripping foot on a pink slipper. She grabs the towel and then goes back inside. It's too cold out there.

She dries herself carefully. Then she opens the door of the shower, feels instantly the difference in temperature and gets used to it slowly, letting the warm air and the cold air mix. The heat and the cold dance around each other, and entwine until they become one.

She stands on her slippers and, without putting them on properly, slides over to the mirror.

She has to go; she knows that.

She dresses in black. Her hair is wet but she doesn't feel like drying it. She opens the draw with Marco's work clothes and takes out his woollen beret. The one she knitted for him, the one with the pompom on top that looks like a panda's tail. It was a Christmas present.

She puts it on. Before going out, she decides to hide the gleam in her eyes behind a black line. She puts make-up on above and below her eyelids, with a quick flick of her wrist.

Now her eyes seem less scared; they have gained a more definite outline. Even her eyes wear their own form of protection – like her body in jumpers that are too large for her, or her nails under their layer of transparent polish.

But it's superficial: only a semblance of protection. She is aware of that.

She fetches her house keys and then a packet of tissues. She pulls out two and puts them in her pocket.

She never allows herself to cry more than two tissues' worth at a time.

She goes out of the house: a small, short building behind the engineering faculty.

A few steps and she's at the bus stop.

She sits down and waits. She can't put it off any longer.

CHAPTER 19

'So, one blow to the head which splattered his brains out. No sign of a struggle. No one heard anything. So there wasn't a fight or an argument. Nothing.'

'Just like before, the victim didn't expect it,' says Marconi.

'What do you mean, like before?' Frolli is always suspicious. Someone who always asks *What am I missing?*

'Two murders in two weeks. In both cases one blow, a dead man, no struggle. In both cases a memento beside the body. The first time the carefully placed razor, wiped clean and closed. The second time the lollipop.'

'Do you mean it's the same murderer?'

'In my opinion, yes. Same height according to forensics, one metre sixty or sixty-five, same force used to strike the fatal blow. A right-handed blow. The print of a stiletto heel, so I'd say we're talking about a woman.'

'A woman!' Frolli bursts out laughing.

Marconi looks at him sullenly. 'In your opinion, is it easier for a man to stay calm, not at all worried, and let himself be caught unawares by another man, possibly big and tall, or by a woman, possibly attractive, and possibly – apparently – defenceless? To explain more clearly: he isn't worried; he believes he's not in any danger.'

'Perhaps the murderer *knew* the victim,' interrupts Tommasi, speaking for the first time.

'Or perhaps *she* should have been the victim.' Marconi is thinking out loud again.

Morini comes in, out of breath, knocking first this time. He doesn't like Frolli, so he's always careful what he says when he's around.

'Excuse me, Inspector.' And he signals for Marconi to come closer.

He sees that Morini's eyes are like golf balls, and he leans forward in a rather theatrical manner.

'That girl – the one from the other day – needs to talk to you urgently,' he says quietly.

This time Marconi doesn't make him repeat it. That conversation could go on for ever, and he's sincerely fed up with meaningless talk that doesn't seem to go anywhere. And, anyway, he likes to think for himself.

A girl? Perhaps even pretty?

'They're waiting for me in my office.' He leaves without saying anything else.

Tommasi mumbles something as well, and follows in the inspector's shadow, leaving Frolli's office with a document in his hand that he's fished out at random from the pile on the desk.

'Hmm,' mutters Frolli, now left alone in the room.

CHAPTER 20

'It's good, this pizza, really light,' says Giulia, reflecting that it's so easily digestible she won't put on an ounce.

'Yes.'

Eva always says very little. She doesn't know what to say when she's with people whose heads are too light.

'Light heads' is a phrase she made up herself. She is convinced that your brain unconsciously picks up the intellectual faculties of the person nearest you, and that whenever you're close to a person with a limited intellect, waves of 'non-thought' invade your space and you end up unable to say anything.

'You know, we joined a gym today.'

Giulia says this in a challenging way. She likes to be in control and Eva's docility always makes her feel good.

She started trying to assert her authority over other people very early on. When she was still a young child, she was already using little tricks to get what she wanted. She told lies. Many were the times she would resort to blackmail to obtain something special, or something beyond her grasp. In fact, the further from her grasp the thing she wanted, the greater the challenge, and therefore the more it was worth trying to get it. By doing this she was able to prove to herself that she was *capable*, that she was equal to the situation. The goal itself wasn't as important as the means, the strategy that she employed to reach her goal.

As Eastern philosophers say, the destination isn't as important as the journey you undertake to get there. Apart from this shared belief, Giulia and Eastern philosophers have very little in common.

She had been especially proud of herself that time when her father refused to buy her a scooter for her to ride to school, given that her school was only five hundred metres from home.

She had cried, stamped her feet and run to her mother, begging her to intercede on her behalf – but nothing doing.

After having expended so much energy and not having had the desired effect, she
understood that she had to forget about traditional methods. She had therefore started to watch her father, to stay as close to him as possible, to spy on him in the moments he spent alone in his study, fondling his mahogany furniture and smoking cigars.

A week later she had gone into his office and had declared, after rubbing her eyes with her knuckles, that she had overheard a telephone call by accident. At that point she burst into tears, pretending that she couldn't go on. He had got up then. 'What is it, sweetie?

73

Tell daddy.' She didn't have to be asked twice. She had overheard a phone call: he was calling some woman 'pussy cat', and was setting up a date at his club. Perhaps he wanted to leave her and her mother.

Her father made sure she found a scooter outside the house the following morning; she had never mentioned the phone call again.

If her mother refused to buy her a new dress because her wardrobe was already stuffed full, or simply because she had bought her something just the week before, without fail she turned on the tears – crocodile tears, switched on as if by remote control. She would claim that she thought herself ugly, that she had no self-confidence, and that this would deter her from eating, so that she could try to look more attractive, because everyone on television says how you have to be thin to be beautiful.

Her desire for posessions grew over the years, and the things she desired became ever more costly: after dolls she moved on to jewels and designer clothes, while the Monopoly money she had loved to keep in her little coral bag with its bright pink plastic handle, when she was nine, was replaced by real banknotes stuffed into her purse together with credit cards borrowed from her parents.

With Eva everything is much simpler. The excuse of the depression from which Giulia is heroically trying to save her troubled friend gives her the right to organise her life, and therefore organise her lunch hour.

Eva goes along with it because she thinks it's better that Giulia thinks she's depressed. That way she doesn't ask any questions and, after all, having her around keeps her distracted.

'Tomorrow we'll start at the gym. I thought that, since my dad is a member – one who never ever *goes* to the gym, obviously, but still a member… Well, it's nearly Christmas, so I've given you his membership as a present. You can do whatever you want. There are aerobics classes, modern dance, even that thing where you kick and punch. You're free to choose what you like. I'll come along with you, and then we'll meet up again after we both finish. I've met this boy who does the massage – Andrea – so I'll be spending my time there, and I'll have a go on the sunbed as well. He's really nice, you know. I think he likes me too, but as I'm going out with Thomas at the moment, the PR person at Ruvido, who's really jealous, I told him that I'll be going to the gym with you, to help you with your depression, so he's OK about it. And, anyway, I'm giving you a great present, aren't I?'

Eva doesn't answer and instead looks at Miew, who's sleeping on her lap.

Giulia isn't happy here. In this flat, which is too small and lacks creature comforts, she doesn't get the attention she needs in order to survive.

'You know, I met a man… a strange guy,' she says, determined to get all the attention she deserves.

'What do you mean, strange?'

'Oh, just totally different. A tough guy, a bit of a misfit.'

Eva doesn't ask her anything else.

It's no fun talking to her, thinks Giulia, now fed up. But then she continues. 'But this one turns me on – quite a lot in fact.'

'Yes?'

'Yes. I'm used to going out with boys, but he's a real man. He knows what he wants, and it just so happens that what he wants now is me.'

Giulia pulls taut the hem of her skirt. She closes her eyes tight for a moment.

'The first evening we met, he was sitting at the bar, on his own, and he was staring at me. We were in Capannina. I don't know what someone like him was doing at Capannina, but that doesn't matter. Then I walked past him to go to the loo.'

She pauses. She raises her eyes from her flowery skirt and glances at her friend, who is playing with the burnt crust of the pizza – just as she was doing five minutes ago when they were talking about the gym.

'I took at least a quarter of an hour to fix my hair and make-up, then I went out – and guess what?'

'I've no idea,' Eva finds a piece of the pizza that's not quite so burnt and puts it in her mouth.

'You've got no imagination. He was there. Leaning against the wall. There wasn't anyone else around. Not a soul. The corridor's long and narrow, and he was there waiting for me, in the dark.'

Eva shivers, and Giulia starts to feel pleased.

'He started to move towards me and I took a step back.'

Eva swallows the pizza.

'He kept on coming towards me. I went back into the bathroom but he came in after me.'

'So what did you do? Didn't you shout for help?'

Giulia is happy now and carries on speaking even more quietly. 'No.'

By now even the cat seems transfixed. Giulia is triumphant.

'I was about to lock myself in the bathroom but he grabbed hold of the door. He came in.'

Eva can't bear it any longer. 'What did you do?' she asks in a whisper.

'He leapt on me, like an animal.'

Eva gives a start and the cat jumps to the floor, astonished, remaining at her feet, with paws outstretched as if she's trying to regain her balance.

Giulia can't stop now. She's enjoying watching Eva's reaction, and wants it to continue watching.

'He put his hand over my mouth to keep me quiet. He had enormous hands.

'Workman's hands?'

'Hands that can't afford to touch a classy woman like me.'

Eva stares.

'He put his tongue in my mouth while he touched my breast with one hand.'

'And you screamed?'

'No, I couldn't. I was in his power.'

Eva has got up, and she starts to pace backwards and forwards. This pacing consumes her. 'What did he do to you, Giulia?' she finally asks.

Giulia decides that she's gone far enough.

'He just looked at me and said "It doesn't end here". He opened the door and he left.'

'But you should have called the bouncers!' Eva cries out, hugging her.

'I can't stop thinking about it,' says Giulia, with a faint smile.

CHAPTER 21

She looks up at him and, for a moment, lights up the room.

With a muted light, it's true, but she lights it up nonetheless. There is no doubt about it.

The identification photographs on the walls.

The mountains of papers dumped on the desk.

The scruffy fake-leather sofa with the faint impression of someone's tired back, like a faded memory.

'Good evening,' she says shyly.

'But it's you!' he answers.

'Do we know each other?'

'No... I don't think so. Sorry, I was mistaken. Tell me why you're here.'

It's the girl I saw in the waiting room. She's not someone I could ever forget. She looks like...

Marconi loses himself for a moment in a memory from long ago and feels that he's back at his school desk.

'I thought about it a lot before coming here,' the girl starts.

She's really beautiful, but not in a flashy way.

'I don't want you to laugh at me – it isn't a joke. I'm saying this now, before I tell you anything, because I know how these things work. I've been through this before.'

I love red hair and hers is naturally red. You can tell by the little freckles on her nose.

'I don't know where to start. I've had a dream, a dream that haunts me,' she explains and waits for the policeman to interrupt her, *And you're here wasting our time because you had a dream?* If he did say that, it would be even more difficult for her to talk.

He doesn't say anything; he just looks at her. Then the girl lowers her gaze and continues with her story.

'I've had these sorts of dreams since I was a child. They're only dreams, but then… then they come true.' She looks up to assess the policeman's reaction. His expression is still hard to read, curious but at the same time lost in who knows what other thoughts.

She isn't wearing any make-up. I don't like girls wearing too much make-up. It's as if they have a veil in front of them. She's beautiful like that, with no make-up – just a very light touch above her eyes. How blue they are. I've never seen such clear blue eyes.

'It feels strange having someone listen to me, like this. Without being interrupted by stupid questions, or by people laughing.'

'Carry on, please.' Now Marconi is now eyeing her breasts; they are hidden under a large black sweater, but you can still see them.

'I feel frightened. Once the dream stops usually…'

Her voice trembles. He would so like to not have to talk.

'Tell me about the dream. Let's start at the beginning.'

'I'm walking. The sun is shining – and it's very bright. Too bright.

'Cars are speeding by me, very fast. I'm aware of being afraid and I start walking quicker.

'Then, all of a sudden, I find myself in an open grey space and I realise. I realise I don't have a shadow any more. But a moment before it was there; it was following me. 'It's disappeared.

'There's a closed door in front of me. It appears suddenly, and I have to open it – because I'm afraid. My shadow has gone and I'm afraid. There's an uneasiness growing inside me.'

Marconi now stops studying the young woman in front of him; he stops tracing her silhouette with his eyes. He just listens to that impassioned, frightened voice. He doesn't yet know exactly what this is about, but a slight shiver runs through him, starting at his feet and spreading upwards until it chokes in his throat. As if he were suddenly standing on ice, with bare feet. Red-hot ice.

'In the end, I open it, that door, and I see it. Blood – blood everywhere. On the walls, on the ground. Everything is stained with blood. And the eyes. Those staring eyes that watch me, looking like they're made out of the blood.'

The girl runs her hands over her legs. Like she's trying to warm up. She is shaking.

Marconi approaches her chair, leans towards her, adopts a softer tone of voice to comfort her, to encourage her. 'How long have you been having these dreams?' he asks her.

'For about a month. But now they've stopped, and that's the problem.'

'The problem?' he repeats.

Yes. When the dreams stop it means that it's happened. I'm never wrong. That's how it works. It's not like any normal dream. I don't know how to explain, but it's different.' She looks up, her eyes full of hope, and again she lights up the room for a moment.

The identification photographs on the walls.

The mountains of papers dumped on the desk.

The shabby fake-leather sofa with the faint impression of someone's tired back, like a faded memory.

'It's as if it's *real*. I feel everything – the warmth of the sun, and the cars, I feel the movement of the air as the cars speed by. But, more than anything else, I feel a hell inside me.

'It's like I'm dying. And then I shake, and sweat, and… I recognise the feeling, because I've had it before. I'd like to be able to pretend these dreams don't mean anything, but I know that's not true. When I have dreams like this, I can see through a door.'

'Don't worry.' Without being aware of it, Marconi starts behaving as if she's a friend.

He would like to touch her. But he doesn't.

'You were right to come here. Leave me your telephone number, then, if I need to ask anything else, I can call you. Everything will be fine, you'll see. Nothing bad's going to happen.'

Marconi hasn't really understood, but he doesn't think that matters. At least he'll have her number.

'But someone's going to die,' she says, raising her voice.

'Lots of people die.' Now he's just a policeman, and he has ruined everything.

CHAPTER 22

Lunch hour at the gym. *Just like the trendy people – I'll be able to tell my sister.* Eva puts on her trainers under her wide black trousers.

She looks around. She would never have thought it would be so busy at this time of day. The changing room is really noisy, with everyone talking loudly, using their microphones. This is another of her inventions, since she imagines that anyone who talks too loudly has a large, invisible microphone, an accessory they always carry with them to whip out whenever they need it.

'Have you seen my new outfit?' Giulia stands on tiptoe and swivels to look at her own arse. Pink, microfibre jogging pants and a matching top.

The girl next to her has a similar outfit in light blue and is pushing up her breasts with her hands inside her bra and pulling down the neckline of her top in order to show off her cleavage. She glances at the pink version of her outfit with a wry smirk.

'You're really sure? The aerobics teacher is

great, and you don't know what you're missing.' Giulia looks at her friend, waiting for an answer – for a change.

'Yes, I'm sure.'

'He really is good. I've lost two kilos in a month with him,' says the girl in blue, who doesn't miss a chance to join in the conversation. 'I'm signed up for two hours a week of aerobics, and one of spinning,' she adds, for the record.

'I don't go to spinning classes any more. It gives you big calves.' Giulia eyes the girl in blue from the knees down.

The girl flounces off, swaying her hips; having apparently not appreciated this intervention from her pink-clad twin. Even Eva heads out of the changing room feeling demoralised. She hates these surroundings. She doesn't feel at ease.

On the raised floor above, a group of Barbie-like girls skip in time. She strides ahead under the gaze of the bodybuilder boys – each one thinking *Look at me. I'm the best-looking. You want me, don't you?* – and there it is, at the end of a maze of muscles and vanity, the kickboxing room.

Black leather bags hanging from the ceiling, with people kicking and punching them. They're mainly men – just two girls: one extremely thin with a wispy ponytail, the other glowing with health and with two long plaits down her back. All that one needs is a horned helmet, and she could be Obelix's wife.

Eva immediately spots the group of new recruits. Frightened eyes and cartoon expressions.

She's fond of a slender young boy with flapping

ears. She's sure that he gets a beating from everyone and would like to learn to defend himself, but, looking at him, she reckons that's going to be hard.

They're already starting, warming up.

The coach looks just like the cartoon character Tigerman, but without the mask.

Eva is soon sweating. She's not at all fit and she's already exhausted after a few minutes. He shouts, to encourage them all to keep going.

Instead of the music now playing throughout the gym – all the rooms are tuned in to a commercial radio station – she would like a nice piece of heavy rock as a soundtrack, perhaps something like that track by Faith No More that she adores, 'The Gentle Art of Making Enemies'. It has always really turned her on, that song.

She would like to start punching and kicking straight away, but she can't. Warm-up, abdominals, exercises on the spot to learn the basic moves: it's not what she wants to do.

She remembers that she was about average in gym classes at school. But even when she was just about average she was fitter than she is now. Perhaps thanks to all those times she had to run so she didn't miss the last bus. Now she's out of breath, every muscle strains and she's thirsty, and, what's more, what is all this effort for? Not even a kick at the bag, and the bag seems to invite it.

The group of old hands nearby do exercises in pairs. They throw punches. One, wearing boxing gloves, lets the punches fly, while as a shield the other uses a big padded cushion, covered in leather.

She can hear the muffled sound, and she's distracted. For a moment she imagines herself in a yellow tracksuit, like Bruce Lee, as the heroine in a fight scene that ends up in a bloodbath, like in *Kill Bill*.

But then the coach makes them lie on the floor as she starts to count out their exercises for the lower abdominals, and Eva, as she does a scissor movement with her legs, is plunged back into a reality of muscles that hurt, and of sweat that runs down her spine and forms beads on her forehead. At the end of the hour she is in pieces, and utterly disappointed.

The showers are all occupied. Steam and chatter that sounds like the buzz of mosquitoes in her ears. Added to everything else, Giulia has just come in, smiling annoyingly.

'We kissed.' She walks towards Eva, singing quietly.

Eva jumps into the first shower that becomes free. She has forgotten her shampoo, as well.

CHAPTER 23

Tommasi is driving. He always puts the seat too far forward when he drives. Although his legs aren't all that long, they form a ridiculous triangle, with his knees almost touching his elbows. His arms, too, are bent unnaturally and seem exceptionally long. He is wearing sunglasses, a pair of fake Ray-Bans.

He is chatting to Marconi, who is gazing out of the window and, because he has pushed his seat back, looks like he is lounging in an armchair at home. Marconi stretches out his legs as far as he can, and with one hand he holds the seatbelt slightly away from his body, as he usually does, because otherwise it's too tight and he feels like he can't breathe properly.

'I don't go out much in the evening. I don't have all that many friends in Bologna,' confesses Tommasi, driving down Viale Masini. 'Work's pretty stressful, and then, what with everything we see every day, you don't much feel like going out, isn't that true?'

'Yes, yes.'

'So, the forensics people have said that it's definitely a woman.'

'Yes.'

A dark-haired boy at the traffic lights at Via Mascarella tries to clean the windscreen. *There's no respect any more for the police.* Marconi waves him away with a gesture of irritation.

'A woman... I don't understand how she did it. It's a real mystery, this case.'

Bologna has changed.

Bologna. The city seems tired, greyer, not as lively.

'Now we know the two murders are linked, your idea's starting to make sense. What was it you called her? The murderer who should've been the victim – something like that?'

'That was it.'

'In fact, that would explain why the two men didn't put up a fight, why there was no sign of a struggle. Yes... it could've happened like you said.'

'It's not just because the victims didn't seem to suspect anything before they were attacked, and therefore didn't try to defend themselves. The most disturbing thing is that the autopsy showed... Keep this quiet, OK? It mustn't go any further.'

'Of course, Inspector.'

'Well, both men had an erection just before they died.'

'What?' Tommasi turns for a second. Shocked, he stares at his superior.

'Careful!' Marconi automatically moves as if to put on the brakes. A young lad on a skateboard has dashed in front of them.

Tommasi brakes hard and the engine cuts out with a thump. 'Fuck it!' He doesn't move: still clutching the steering wheel, with his foot still pressed down on the brake.

They stay motionless for a moment while the boy disappears down a narrow street on their right, without apologising or even looking back at them.

'I don't believe it. Look at that moron!'

'And if some poor sod knocks one of them over, they even have to pay them compensation.'

'These kids have no respect for anything or anyone. They have everything they want right from when they're born, and look how they end up. They just don't know how to behave any more.'

A car behind them sounds its horn, not realising that the stationary vehicle is a police car.

'There's no respect any more for the police. Did I already say that?'

Tommasi starts off again but soon they stop for a coffee. The barista at Settimo Cielo is a short man with a friendly face, a true local accent, and an overwhelming desire to grumble.

'Two coffees.'

'Another robbery in broad daylight in the centre of the city the other day. Where's it all going to end?' he grumbles, reaching for the cups.

'Come on, don't start. We do our job. But there aren't enough of us – and we're not paid enough,' Tommasi responds. He already knows the *barista*'s views.

'I'm not saying you don't do your job. I'm just saying that, with all these immigrants, you aren't safe leaving the house.'

'Don't start on immigrants again,' Tommasi blurts out. He is originally from Naples, and remembers when he was little and he was the foreigner. At school the other boys said his father had come to steal work from Italians, as if Naples was another country.

'I can't afford to be a liberal,' says the *barista*, as he puts the two steaming cups in front of them and goes back to drying the tall glasses, the ones used for prosecco.

'What were you saying before, Inspector?' Tommasi is annoyed. His eyebrows seem like they meet in the middle even more than normally.

'This is confidential information. So I'm warning you – not a word to anyone.'

Tommasi leans forward, ready to digest this tasty bit of information.

'So, both men were hard before they died.'

'Which means that the stiletto print could be...?'

'Yes, that footprint could belong to the murderer. And it also means that the first statement we got from the woman at the service station could contain an element of truth. The blonde, sexy woman – perhaps she wasn't a real babe, like the woman described her, but everything else could fit.'

'The lollipop next to the second victim made me think of a woman straight away. I couldn't see the victim himself eating a lollipop. Not someone like him, I mean.'

'Picture the scene,' says Marconi, changing tack. 'In the first murder, he pushes her into the bathroom. He wants to fuck her, he's looking forward to it, and she doesn't allow him time to realise anything's wrong before she cuts his throat.

'Then the second murder. It's late at night and she lets herself be followed to that garbage dump. His intentions are definitely not honourable, but he's not worried. He knows he's stronger than her. There's no contest: it's as good as done. But she hits him with a heavy object – a club or perhaps an iron bar. She smashed his head open with two blows and it was all over quickly. I've looked at the photos again.'

'And?'

'And they've both got the same expression. The expression of someone who's just landed in the shit.'

'I could be wrong, but the last one, Mario Rossi...'

'Yes, like in those adverts: "There's always a Mario Rossi."'

'He used to beat his wife.'

'That's right. The man was violent: We've got two complaints on file from his first wife. But now he was with a Romanian. They were living together in a block of flats in Via Casini.'

They get up and go over to pay.

'It's on me.' The *barista* turns towards them. 'Let's see if it wakes you lot up a bit,' he adds under his breath.

'What?'

'Have a good day,' he says, shrugging his shoulders.

'Morning. Police.'

Silence.

'You heard me. Open the door.' Marconi doesn't bother trying to sound polite. 'Open the door. We don't have all day.'

Silence.

'Open the door. We only want to ask you a few questions. Or, if you prefer, we can come back later and do a search, and then you'll be screwed.'

The door opens as if by magic.

The girl turns her back on them and goes back into the living room, or rather a minute kitchen that's also used as a living room. It contains an enormous television set, switched on but with the sound turned off.

There's a strong smell of fried food.

She sits down. It looks like she's only just out of her teens. A washed-out blonde wearing a pair of tight jeans and a synthetic red jersey top.

'What do you want?'

'Tell me about Mario.'

'I didn't know him very well.'

'But you live in his flat?'

'I've been here for two months. I do the cleaning and in return he let me stay here.'

'The cleaning?' echoes Tommasi.

'His ex-wife informed us you were living here. Yet you haven't even bothered to get in touch with us. You do know that he's dead, don't you?'

'She's mad, that woman. Yes, I know, I know. I saw it on TV but I don't know anything, and anyway, what am I supposed to do. I only do his cleaning. I don't know anything.'

'You already said you don't know anything.'

Marconi leans against the table and crosses his legs.

'Sit down. Would you like a drink?' she says, clearly used to making men feel at ease.

'No,' Marconi replies with an air of incorruptibility.

He nearly loses his balance and plants both feet back flat on the ground.

'He used to go out every night and come back late. I don't really know anything else.'

'Did he drink? Do drugs? Anyone threaten him? What was his relationship like with his ex-wife?'

'She's mad. Once she kept ringing the bell and shouting "You tart, open the door. You're not taking all my maintenance money." She's mad.'

'And then?'

'And then I don't know *anything*. I've already told you,' she pouts. He could tell how she usually got whatever she wanted with that pout.

But it doesn't work with me, Marconi thinks. 'Talk, or there'll be trouble.' Spoken as if he were in a film. 'The murderer's a woman, about your height. So it'll be better for you if you co-operate, or you'll end up on our list of suspects.'

'I'm hardly the only woman one metre sixty tall.' She smiles. 'Do what you want. I don't know anything. And this isn't my flat – I'm just a cleaner. I've already told you everything I know.'

She's really not bad, not beautiful but put her in a miniskirt...

'OK, but we may need to talk to you again,' adds Tommasi, before the inspector can let slip something else about the case.

'Hello?'

'They've been here... I didn't say anything. I'll see you tonight at the usual place.'

CHAPTER 24

'Are you going out again tonight?'
'Yes, I told you. Do you think I work just to keep you comfortable? I need to have a bit of fun as well, don't I?'

'It's just that we don't spend enough time together, and I don't like that. I'm scared we'll drift apart,' says Viola, downcast.

'You know I always want to make love to you. Do you think I'd feel like that if I was going off you?' Marco spanks her on the buttocks as she clears the table.

'I'd like the two of us to go out together sometimes, just you and me.'

'Listen, Viola, I've already told you, so there's no point pretending not to hear me whenever it suits you. I need my own space. I need to spend some time with my friends. I already feel tied down... And you know how I get jumpy.'

'But are you tired of me?'

Marco gets up from his chair.

'You *know* you're my little pumpkin; I'll never get tired of you.' He hugs her and gives her a kiss on the neck.

'But now I've got to get ready, otherwise I'll be late.'

Viola follows him like a pet dog. She sits down on the bed and watches him.

She thinks Marco is so good-looking. He isn't very tall, but that's OK. Swarthy, with dark eyes and a beautiful smile. It was his smile that she fell in love with. And she fell in love with the way he half-closes his eyes when he grins, and how a dimple appears on the left side of his mouth.

Marco lost his head over her tits and arse; but he always claims he fell in love with Viola because she's as sweet as icing sugar.

He puts on a pair of ripped jeans, a white V-neck T-shirt and white trainers. Then he goes into the bathroom to put gel in his hair.

She follows him, lowers the toilet seat and sits down.

'Don't wait up for me. And tomorrow I'm doing the second shift, so I'll be late.'

'Where are you going tonight?'

'Nowhere special, but don't wait up. I might stop at Claudio's and have a game on his PlayStation.'

Viola sits huddled up on the toilet seat and plays with her toes, thinking how she would like to go out every now and then, too. But she doesn't want to make a fuss.

'You're overdoing the aftershave! You're not trying to impress some girl, are you?'

'What girl? You're the only one for me.'

Marco leans over and kisses her on the top of her head. 'Night-night, pumpkin.'

'Wait a minute.'

But he has already closed the door behind him.

She stays sitting on the white toilet seat. She suddenly feels heavy. Heavy inside. In her heart.

She rubs her eyes with the backs of her hands until she sees flashes of blue light, like she used to do when she was small. She stretches herself and then goes back to playing with her toes.

Did I do the right thing, talking to that cop? She doesn't like to call him a 'cop': it sounds rather like an insult. But that's what he is, a cop.

She gets up and goes to stand in front of the large mirror on the wall in the corridor. She adores that mirror. There's no frame, just a reflecting surface. And it makes her look thinner, and makes her seem taller as well. She takes off her vest and lets it fall to the floor.

Ugly thoughts. *Again.* They spread throughout her, running backwards and forwards along her nerves, inside her veins, under her fingernails. They drive through her like needles until they take root inside her like some sort of demonic creature, beneath her skin.

How she would like to stop herself thinking, to stop tormenting herself.

To fill the emptiness she feels inside, every time she is on her own.

She can't live without a man.

She's cold. The demonic creature is calling her by name. *Viola. I know you can hear me, Viola...*

She opens the drawer of the bedside table, reaches under the notebooks and pulls out a flick knife with a six-inch, stainless-steel blade.

She snaps it open and feels the coldness of it between her fingers.

It's sharp as a razor, and has been scorched with a lighter.

CHAPTER 25

The porcelain doll is dressed as a geisha. She looks stunning in the long silk dress, black with red flowers, long splits at both sides which give a glimpse of her perfect legs. She has put up her hair with a metal hairpin that ends in two red jewels. They're like glittering drops of blood, holding back her hair on a level with her temples.

Her neck is immaculate, snow-white, as perfect as a work of art sculpted by skilled hands that have managed to create a harmonious balance between fragility and perfection.

She is leaving the club where she has been dancing, lulled by the dark electro-pop music there. In the club, she looked around until she spotted a young woman. Attractive, Mediterranean-looking, long black hair and curvaceous. She slowly, imperceptibly, moved closer to her. Step by step. Then she started to move in front of her. Dancing, looking into her eyes.

A dance of seduction.

The girl let herself be seduced, and soon they found themselves kissing passionately on a small sofa, under the aroused gaze of the passers-by. People couldn't help but look at them, two lustful Venuses, tongues entwined, sensuously caressing each other through their clothes.

They disappeared into the bathroom and were gone for about forty minutes. Then the white Venus fixed her lipstick and now here she is walking down the street, leaving a trail of perfume, as seductive as it is dangerous.

Soon she realises that she's being followed. She hears footsteps echoing behind her, but she doesn't turn round. Not yet.

She starts walking more quickly, then she starts to run, but her steps are restricted, the too-tight dress making it difficult to move freely.

She finds herself in a dead end. A wall rising in front of her. An abandoned scooter that has lost its wheels. A cat miaowing at the invisible moon, as if upset by the light of the street lamps.

Now she turns and looks behind her. There are two men. Dark skin and white teeth. The tall one has a knife in his hand, the other keeps opening and closing his fingers as if he's imagining touching her, holding her.

With a very thick accent, the one with the knife tells her not to shout for help. She doesn't shout, but she moves back. She opens her small sequined clutch bag.

'We don't want your money, love. Not yet,' says the taller man. He has a few days' growth of beard and eyes so narrow they look like they're closed.

They start laughing.

Crack.

Crack.

Two pistol shots.

Two bodies lying on their backs. The blood of one merges with the blood of the other in a macabre dance of bodily fluids.

One is still alive. He moans and starts to drag himself towards the pavement.

High heels echo behind him. Now she is beside him.

He turns to mumble something; she doesn't let him get a look at her.

She takes the hairpin from her hair and drives it into his eye, punching through to his brain.

She cleans the blood off the red jewel onto the man's trousers, and puts the hairpin back in her hair. She takes one last look at the scene.

A beautiful still life.

CHAPTER 26

'Come on, that's it. Push those legs. Put your back into it. That's better.'

The coach watches her, satisfied. His star pupil, Eva, has only been coming to his classes for a couple of months but she's really taken to it. A little lioness. But he never pays her compliments; he's afraid that she'll stop putting so much effort into it, that she'll become big-headed.

He really likes this girl. She's different from all the others. She's plucky, she doesn't like to show off, she's modest and shy; and, on top of all that, she's the only one who's willing to exercise with Patrick, the thin boy with ears that stick out, who is truly hopeless. Instead of hitting the glove when they all do exercises in pairs, he often hits his partner in the face. He lacks co-ordination, he's a disaster, but she hasn't let him give up. She says to him: 'You can do it. You just need a bit more patience, and the day you do it right, you'll feel great.'

Patrick listens to her with his mouth half open and his eyes wide, as if he is trying to focus on her every single word. And he doesn't give up. He doesn't want to give up because he wants to change his life.

He hates Stefano, the boy in the fifth form who's a thug and beats up everyone else at school. He hates him because Stefano often steals his packed lunch, he is always shoving him, and more than once he has pushed him over. He once made him miss the bus home, holding him back by his jacket. He makes him salute when he goes past. He threw his exercise book down the toilet.

Above all, he hates him because he insults his mother.

He says she's a slut. It upsets Patrick just to think about it, that word, used in connection with his mother.

Stefano says that the slut must have fucked a sick mouse to have produced such an ugly son.

It's wrong for people to speak ill of his mother, because she's not here any more. No one should disrespect her. No one.

In fact, it was when Stefano insulted his mother that Patrick tried to rebel and ended up getting a serious beating. Those other things he can put up with, but not when it's about his mother. No one can insult her; they should let her rest in peace.

One day I'll make him pay. I'll shut his mouth and mum will be proud of me, watching from up there.

Eva also imagines looking into the eyes of one specific person: it's always him she sees in front of her when she hits the punchbag hard. The unknown man who wanted to hurt her, and who robbed her: the one who took away her happiness, forever. Eva never smiles; she is stubbornly solemn. But now she knows how to kick properly, and her right hook makes sparks fly.

You can't touch me, you bastard. You can't touch me. You can't touch me. And she throws herself back into pummelling the punchbag.

CHAPTER 27

The car is parked in the dark. Anyone would think it was empty if it weren't for the steamed-up windows.

The boy in the white T-shirt has his hand on the girl's head.

The hand moves backwards and forwards.

Every now and then he lets out a moan. The sound of an animal in heat.

'You're good,' he says through his teeth.

He's about to come. The moment before coming, he always thinks about her – at home, waiting for him in their bed.

He enjoys the thought.

'Here, this is for you.' He holds the envelope out to the girl, who is wiping her mouth on her arm.

'Thanks.' She hides the envelope between her breasts.

'You know that I'm always good to girls who are good to me.'

The car drives off.

It leaves an empty space. A dry space.

Everywhere else is wet. The rain is falling in light drops, like thoughts that come and go.

A small pale rectangle is left, that gradually colours with dark spots.

It disappears.

Like youth.

CHAPTER 28

The phone rings and breaks the silence.

'Yes?'

'This is Mrs Balugani. I live in the flat below you. You might remember me.'

'Of course I remember you.' *What does that old woman want from me*, thinks Viola, and smiles.

'I had to call you. I didn't straight away because I said to myself, they're young, perhaps it'll only happen this once. But then it's happened too often – you have your music on so loud, even when other people should be asleep. Don't think this is all my own idea, calling you – the other tenants have been complaining about it too.'

'I'm sorry, I didn't think that –'

'The music is deafening. My bedroom is right under your living room, and after lunch I have a lie down because of my health. And then in the evening as well, at a certain point I need to go and rest, but then you start with that noise and...'

'I had no idea. I'm sorry...'

'I've been patient so far but...'

'As I said, I'm really sorry.'

'It's not just me saying this, don't think it is... The fact is, the others talk behind your back, but I'd rather speak to you in person. And don't think that I've got anything against you two. I know you're just youngsters.'

'Of course not. It won't happen again.'

'I knew you were a well mannered girl who would understand, not like that woman on the first floor. Do you know what she did?'

'Erm... no, I can't say I do.'

'She bought herself a dog without asking anyone's permission.'

'I don't think you have to ask permission any more to –'

'Whether that's true or not, it's a matter of good sense, I'd say, living in a flat. Anyway, she left the dog outside in the communal garden, did you know that?'

'Yes, but it's a small dog.' Viola would like to have a dog. She would shower it with affection. She has never owned a dog; she hasn't even had a cat. Not even a canary.

'Do you know that dogs' urine is acid? The plants die. Haven't you seen the pansies? Burnt! Dogs' urine is corrosive – it burns plants – and who's going to pay for new ones? They were so pretty. Without getting any thanks from anyone, I used to water them myself. What can one do, that's what I'm asking myself, what can one do...?'

'I'm sorry, but I have to go now.'

'But what do you have to go and do? I know you don't work, and you don't have children.'

'I have to go and... make the dinner.'

'I'm sorry for disturbing you, then, if you still have to make dinner. I was just speaking on behalf of the tenants. Everyone ought to be a bit more interested in any problems affecting us all.'

'Bye.'

'Goodbye.'

Viola is now exhausted. She throws herself onto the sofa and surrenders herself to the embrace of the cushions. She thinks about the burnt pansies, *viole del pensiero*. It seems like an omen. Viola in the midst of her thousand thoughts. Burnt.

She thinks about how she didn't even finish school. In the third year she was kept back and then she'd met Marco. Or perhaps she met Marco and then in the third year she decided to stop and to just acquire a diploma as a business secretary.

She knows how to type OK. She doesn't ever read books, just magazines. *Glamour* is the one she likes best. She can cook, but what else? Her boyfriend goes out every night, so she isn't even much good as a wife. If only she were a wife! Not that he will ever marry her.

Viola would like to get married. In a white dress.

She can picture a white dress, tight at the waist. She imagines herself with her hair up and little roses in it.

She wears nice make-up, like the models in her magazines.

He is waiting for her at the altar. There are flowers everywhere, and lots of smiling people.

She realises that she is crying.

It won't happen.

It will never happen, and that hurts her. Inside.

If only she had a dog. Or at least a canary.

CHAPTER 29

'This evening you're having dinner at my house. I've already organised everything, and I've told them we're going to the pictures. But, instead, I'm seeing Luca.'

'I can't, Giulia. I'd love to but –'

'Miew's invited too. I've got fish specially for her.'

I don't believe it, even dinner for Miew? And only because last time I said no, because otherwise Miew would be left at home on her own.

'I'll expect you at eight, on the dot,' she adds bossily.

Eva doesn't like going out in the evening. She's scared of the dark, of what might be hiding under its dark-blue mantle.

'OK.'

CHAPTER 30

Marconi looks out at the rain from his armchair. The chair has its back turned to the kitchen and the front door.

It doesn't give a damn, his armchair, it leaves everything behind.

He looks out.

He thinks about the girl with red hair.

He thinks about her sad eyes, so blue. So light that they hurt.

His mobile phone is resting on his right leg.

His left leg, stretched out unnaturally, rests on the radiator.

It's too high there to be comfortable, but he likes sitting like this.

He would like to pick up the phone, dial ten numbers, just ten, and then he could hear her voice. But he can't do that.

He wouldn't have anything to say, and then… He can't do it, that's all there is to it.

But he would like to.

He likes women.

Mysterious creatures. Fragrant.

He likes women's eyes.

He feels that hidden in the depths of a woman's eyes is a whole other world.

Perhaps a world inhabited by everything they've seen with those eyes.

His mother had lifeless, tired eyes.

She had seen too much shit during her life, and in the end that was all she had left to fill the emptiness of her dark eyes.

He was a child, and a child can't fill that emptiness.

A child can only see what's right in front of his nose.

A child only sees as far as the things he needs.

This child had seen her for the last time as she sat on the bench in front of their house on that sweltering Wednesday. The same sweltering Wednesday that sometimes comes back to haunt him in those nights when it rains or it's too dark. Just like this one. She had her apron tied around her waist and that same look in her eyes. He didn't understand what those eyes were trying to say. When he did understand, it was too late.

He has never understood women.

He thinks about the murderer.

A woman. Definitely fragrant.

Beautiful. In fact, stunning.

He thinks about what they must have thought, the men who saw her standing there in front of them a moment before they died.

It started raining again a while ago. Yet more rain.

Like tears.

The telephone rings.

I'll be there straight away.

CHAPTER 31

Giulia lives in a huge house in the Saragozza area of the city.

As she rings the doorbell, Eva – the cat box in her hand – watches the glittering snake of lights leading towards San Luca. The light radiates up into the sky. It's a reassuring sight. Miew lets out a miaow; she's uncomfortable and she's grumbling.

The lock on the side gate clicks open. The gate is wrought iron, painted black, and matches the other, much larger, automatic gates and the railings that look like long eyelashes silhouetted against eyes lit up by a yellow light.

Her slight, dark shadow crosses the well tended garden. The shapes of trees appear out of the darkness, their branches curving so that they look like trees in an oriental painting.

'Daddy, this is my friend Eva,' Giulia says, sounding rather like a pimp.

Her father, about sixty, hair thinning but well groomed, and dressed in grey Armani, has a hint of a smile that looks more like a grimace, lighting up his face with an ambiguous light.

'Eva, this is my mother. Isn't she beautiful?'

'Yes,' lies Eva, and can't help noticing that the woman has had plastic surgery to her nose, mouth and presumably her breasts, and thinking that soon the same thing will be done to the daughter.

The dinner begins. A fish starter: a risotto with seafood comprising lots of strangely named sea creatures liberally doused in white wine.

Miew is being treated like a VIP, on the floor, next to the table. She is eating salmon from a gilded saucer but, judging from her expression, she would much prefer her usual toxic croquettes.

'Usually we don't allow animals in the dining room, but Giulia insisted. It has been vaccinated, your cat, hasn't it?' asks Giulia's mother.

'Of course. And she's clean – she sleeps with me,' says Eva, wishing that she could say *No, she's got scabies*, just to see how she would react.

Dotted around the room are valuable rugs, porcelain and glittering silverware, enormous still-life paintings. This room wouldn't look out of place in a castle.

Eva, lost in wonder, looks at a threadbare picture in a gold frame. It depicts peasants bending over, while sowing their crops.

'It's beautiful, isn't it?' says Giulia's father.

'Yes, very beautiful. I've never seen anything so big.'

Everyone laughs.

'It looks very old,' Eva adds, embarrassed.

'It's a tapestry, from 1860. It belonged to a noble

Spanish family that lived for a while here in Bologna. I bought it at an auction. Giuliacci wasn't ready to let it slip through his hands, but in the end I bid enough to leave him standing. Just think...'

'You shouldn't talk about money at the table, dear.'

'You're right, dear,' and he dabs at his mouth with his napkin, as if to wipe away the sum of money that he was going to disclose to her.

Miew seems bewildered by the suffocating atmosphere and by such a vulgar show of wealth. She jumps on to a piece of furniture, wood with an ochre grain, endangering the safety of a cut-glass vase.

'Oh, please. That vase came from my mother's collection. Stop that animal now!' cries the mother without, moving her silicon lips.

The cat looks at her defiantly and starts to purr, rubbing herself against the vase.

'It's worth more than the two of you put together. Stop that animal!'

'Got her,' says Eva with the cat in her arms. 'She was just playing. She's never broken anything at home.'

'And I was only joking, what I said. I can't even remember exactly what I said,' the mother giggles nervously.

After dinner Giulia starts to show her round the house. It would be more appropriate to call it a museum. Antiques, collections of everything worth collecting, and finally her room.

She carries a bunch of enormous keys, like Bluebeard. And she boasts about having made copies of even the 'forbidden' keys, because every now and then she likes to readjust her pocket money.

Hers is truly a room for a princess: a four-poster

bed with yards of pink taffeta curtains, silk sheets, and ornaments everywhere. Photographs with Giulia in close-up and full-length, her head turned to the right, then to the left; now smiling, now serious. But always artfully posed.

'Now, let's go' Giulia says. 'I can't stand your cat when it miaows like that. You wouldn't expect me to let it run around loose in here, would you? And anyway, Luca's expecting me. Remember, if anyone asks, I've been with you all this evening,' Giulia says.

'No problem. It's not as if anyone ever asks me anything anyway.'

'Yes, but if anyone does, I've been with you. Say you'll say so, or I'll be upset.'

'Yes, yes,' repeats Eva.

'Thanks, you're a star!' and Giulia hugs her on impulse. 'Oh, by the way, you're looking a bit muscly, you know. Your arms – it's revolting. You shouldn't overdo the gym, or you'll end up looking like a man.'

CHAPTER 32

'How many times have I told you?' He glares angrily at her. 'I don't want you going through my things. I don't want you wearing my jumpers, my socks or any other fucking thing of mine, do you understand?'

'It's just that I feel comfortable in them.' Viola stretches out her arms to show how good she looks in the jumper a couple of sizes too big for her.

'Viola, I've told you time and again. You need a jumper, buy yourself one. You're not short of money. But I don't want you using my things. I just don't want you to. It drives me mad. And I don't want you going through my wardrobe.'

'But I have to open the wardrobe to put your things away after I've ironed them...'

'No excuses. Socks the other day, today my jumper. How can I make you understand?'

'But what harm is there?'

'Wash my things and put them on the chair, like I told you. I want to put them away where *I* want. If you do it I can't find anything. You know that. You've got your own wardrobe, I've got mine. You've got your things, and I've got mine. I don't pinch your things and put them on. And your perfume gets on everything you use, and I smell like a whore.'

'But Marco, what harm is there if I use one of your jumpers. This one's old and you never wear it, and it's black and you don't wear black...'

He comes closer to her as if to hit her. He raises his hand.

'Do you want the fucking jumper? Take the fucking thing. I hate it, I hate it, and I hate you when you're wearing it. But never go in my wardrobe again. I won't tell you another time.' His hand is still raised, like a threat.

Viola can't lift her gaze from the floor.

He told her he hated her. She heard him, he really said it: that he hated her like he hates this shapeless jumper, with its pulled threads and its signs of wear and tear.

He has now turned away from her. He sits down on the sofa and switches on the TV.

Viola can't speak.

As always happens, her head is throbbing with words, but she isn't able to say them out loud. They cry out inside her, but her mouth is sealed shut. *I miss you! That's why I go in your wardrobe and search through your T-shirts and shirts. I'm looking to see if there's a little piece of you left behind, even among your socks. Then I find something that seems to still have your smell, and I put it on and it feels like you're here with me.*

It hurts, that voice in her head; it screams. It screams so much it hurts, but it doesn't make a sound.

'What's for dinner? I'm hungry, and I have to go to work, in case you've forgotten.'

CHAPTER 33

'What have we got here?' asks Marconi, pushing up his collar. Tommasi is standing opposite him, and a shrug of his shoulders indicates that he doesn't know anything yet.

Marconi has known Tommasi for two years. At the beginning, they worked together and that was all, like with everyone else: the usual relationship between an inspector and his junior officer. Then, gradually, he started to notice Tommasi's skills and character.

A very attentive lad, with a burning desire to learn, who always followed a step behind and was always there, watching his back, like that time when there was a robbery in the supermarket in Via del Borgo San Pietro.

Marconi hadn't spotted the accomplice who was acting as look-out, and was waiting there in the parked Fiat. And, when the others had escaped in an old VW Golf, he would have got himself run over if it hadn't been for Tommasi, his shadow, who had pushed him out of the way just in time.

They had looked at each other without saying

anything, but from that day on Marconi had become much more aware of him. He noticed how he had chestnut-coloured eyes, with hair the same colour, and that he raised his lips on one side when he smiled.

At the police station, the other officers used to call them 'mother goose' and 'baby goose' – not in their hearing of course. If he had overheard them, Marconi would have been really pissed off, and when he's pissed off everyone knows it.

One of the men from forensics is measuring the distance between the two bodies. The other bends over with silver-coloured, slightly curved forceps and picks up something that he then puts into a clear envelope.

Marconi takes a step forward. He's known Galliera for years, so knows that there's nothing to worry about. He doesn't bite.

'How's it going?'

'We're getting there. What do you want to know, Inspector?'

'What can you tell me so far?'

'So far, the details are fairly vague, but, as you can see, there were two shots from a small calibre pistol. One dead instantaneously. The other dragged himself to the pavement and was finished off by a violent blow with some pointed object. Perhaps a screwdriver. It went right through one eye and into his skull. I've just picked up a small, red glass jewel that was lying by the side of the second victim. Nothing else, so far. Now let me finish off here. I've got a wife waiting for me at home.'

Marconi pretends not to have heard that last bit.

He pretends not to remember that he himself has got no one waiting for him at home.

'No one heard anything, as usual, I suppose?' he asks, turning to Tommasi.

'It's a cul-de-sac, as you can see. There's only that old falling-down building and then at the end there's a wire fence that backs on to an abandoned field. On the other side, at the far end of the street, there's a bar, a kind of social club. One of those places that plays strange music – I don't know what you call it – where strange people go, with weird hair, all dressed in black.' He tries to explain what he means by waving his hands.

'Has anyone been into the club to ask questions?'

'No, it was too late. It was almost dawn when the boy found them both. He says he came out of there to throw up and then he started to walk about to get a breath of fresh air. He's a minor, so they took him to the station. Someone will have taken his statement before his parents came to fetch him.'

'Nothing else unusual?'

'Do you mean erections? Because, if you do, you'll have to ask them. But I think they'll only be able to tell you after they've examined the bodies.'

'What are you talking about? No. What I meant was is there any souvenir left this time?'

'I don't think so. But then they haven't talked to me yet,' and he indicates the two people dressed like astronauts, who are now showing signs of having finished.

'Thanks for calling me. I hate being at home when these things happen.'

'I did what you told me. Even if Frolli didn't like it much.'

CHAPTER 34

Eva looks out of the car window. She's driving slowly, with music playing in the background. She's slightly tense but she was expecting to feel worse. For the first time in six months she's going home, to Ravenna.

To face her fears she has to visualise them. She's doing that now. The terror she feels making that journey again is like facing one of her partners at training: a potential aggressor that she has to keep at a distance. As she has learned to do. Today her coach told her that she's ready to fight in a match, if she wants to.

Perhaps because, during the exercises in pairs, she knocked Brando over. She gave him such a powerful kick that everyone turned to look. The feeling she had when she saw him on the ground, at her feet, holding his side because of the pain was tremendous. She felt alive, excited, carried away by a new fire burning inside her.

Tomorrow is her birthday and Giulia has asked what she'd like for it. Nothing. She doesn't want anything. But that's not really true: she would like the only present she can never have. To forget.

'Come on, open mine first,' says Elisa, 'I can't wait for you to see what it is. Hurry up.'

The small rectangular parcel from her sister has a pink flower on it; her mother's is larger and conceals something soft, probably a hand-knitted jumper, her usual present. Occasionally she rings the changes with a scarf, always painstakingly knitted by hand.

It's her bad luck to have her birthday in the winter and to have a mother obsessed with making things...

Then there's an envelope from her father. Every year he prefers to give her money, adding, without fail, 'So you can buy something you'd like'.

'Hurry up. Open mine.'

'OK.' Eva tears off the paper. A silver-coloured box. 'Red Passion' in embossed letters.

'But it's a lipstick. I don't wear lipstick.'

'Exactly. You're twenty-four and it's time you started to, otherwise you'll never find a boyfriend,' Elisa says, beaming.

Her sister loves lipsticks, make-up, face creams and everything else that's supposed to make a woman beautiful. Their mother used to tell her off when she was small, because she would steal her lipstick. Her mother she never used it herself, anyway, except on special occasions. When Elisa did put on lipstick, she always ended up with it everywhere: on her lips, rubbed on her cheeks, and even on her eyelids instead of eye shadow. Then, still vividly coloured, she would deny having any make-up on.

'It's a good brand. I spent all my savings. The sales

girl recommended it; red is the colour that suits blondes best, she told me; and it's one of those that moisturises as well.'

'Are you going into advertising as well, when you grow up, Eli?' asks Eva, amused.

'No, I'm going to be a model!' her little sister replies, without any trace of doubt. 'Try it on!' she says, jumping up and down.

Elisa is beautiful. She has very long hair, blonde with copper-coloured highlights. Her eyes are green, almond-shaped, with extremely long lashes. Her lips are thin, unlike the fleshy lips of her sister.

And she has a small, cute, turned-up nose. Eva smiles, remembering that, when they were little, she used to pretend to steal it, showing Elisa the tip of her thumb between her index and middle fingers, just like the nuns at nursery had taught her to do.

'No, give it back,' her baby sister would then cry. 'You're horrible! Give it back!'

Now, she still jumps up and down like she used to. 'Go on, try it!'

Eva stands in front of the large mirror that greets guests coming into the hall.

The lipstick, she slides it over her lips. She gives them colour. She stands still, looking at her reflection.

'You're so beautiful!' Elisa exclaims.

Eva opens her eyes wide and immediately wipes off the lipstick with one hand.

'Why did you do that? You've ruined it. It looks like blood on you now.'

Eva moves away from the mirror. She can't look at herself any more.

CHAPTER 35

The area is always the same. Marconi uses a felt-tip pen to write on a torn map. On it are marked the places where the Black Widow has struck.

'The only thing that the dead men have in common is the fact that they're – how shall I put it? – rather violent. She's like a spider: she weaves her web, she prepares everything carefully, then she lets herself be followed. She knows how to make a man follow her, and make him fall into her trap. She doesn't attack; with her it's always defence, but premeditated.'

'How can you know that?' asks Frolli, from behind him. 'I think this is all bloody stupid, and the *questore* will require something more than just guesswork. I've covered your arse this time, but next time you go yourself and explain what we've got after more than three months of investigations. Fuck all, that's what we've got.'

'The second victim had a record of domestic violence; but the first time the complaint was withdrawn. And then the last two we've known for some time. They used to sell drugs in the area behind Palestro – in the clubs as well.'

'So what? What does it prove? Nothing. It proves *nothing*.'

'Well, I've thought about it over and over. About that lollipop still being in its wrapper. She wanted to say that she hadn't let him have it. Understand?'

'What the fuck are you talking about? So I'll tell the *questore*: "She hadn't let him have it." Thank you. I feel much happier now. We've kept the press quiet. No statement. Cases not linked. But the odd bit of information has leaked out – I don't know how – and now they want a press conference. Do you understand, or do I have to spell it out for you? So you'd better prepare something to say.'

'I'll explain more clearly. She didn't let him "unwrap" her – to have her, in other words. Next to the dead man was the untouched lollipop. He wanted to have her and she didn't let him. It doesn't seem that difficult to me. Pop psychology. The lorry driver had undone the last button on his trousers. Same thing: he followed her into the bathroom and perhaps even tried to assault her, but she killed him. And the same with these two.'

'But how can you be so sure? At scenes of attempted sexual assault there are signs of a struggle... but what am I doing talking to you? Look, I'm washing my hands of this. You can handle the *questore*.'

'Yes, but this isn't our usual attempted sexual assault. It's the woman who provokes the men, to make them follow her. She makes them think that everything's fine, that they're the hunters, but in fact she's the one who's planning everything. And then she kills them, by surprise. It was like that this time as well. They were two pushers. One had already been inside for a month, for sexual assault on a minor in the car park of a disco last summer. What do you think they wanted from her?'

'But this time there's no evidence that links the two dead men to her. Just a piece of glass, and anyone could have lost that. It could easily be another drug dealer that killed them.'

'Yes, with a semi-automatic. Wait.' He opens the crime lab's report. 'It was probably a six-calibre gun, an old model that nowadays would be considered a collector's piece.'

'So, you're linking it to the razor, isn't that a bit of a stretch? Facts – just tell me what facts there are. I'm waiting.'

The photograph of the teddy bear in the blood, staring out with its small glass eyes.

'Fuck, why didn't I think of this before! Let's check that type of pistol. All the pistols registered here and in the surrounding areas.'

'What the fuck?'

Marconi is already out in the corridor. 'Tommasi, you and I are going to that disco tonight. Just wear black, otherwise they won't let us in,' he adds, before heading out under the grey sky.

CHAPTER 36

He rings the doorbell. No answer. He starts to worry that there's no one home, but then he hears a noise from inside the house. He rings again. He needs to see her.

'Who is it?' asks a faint voice.

'Excuse me, I'm Inspector Marconi. Can you open the door, please?'

'Wait a minute while I get dressed.'

The thought that she is naked on the other side of the door makes him feel hot. Marconi leans against the door; he's slightly out of breath. To give himself time to calm down, he has walked up the stairs, but he's not as fit as he used to be.

Viola hurries; she slips on Marco's black jumper and cleans the blood off the blade with a few sheets of loo roll that she then throws into the toilet. She flushes. She hides the knife again in its usual drawer. She pulls off the elastic hair band with purple plastic butterflies, and leaves her hair hanging loose as she rushes to open the door.

'Sorry. I'd just come out of the shower,' she mumbles.

He takes a step forward. 'Can I come in?'

'Of course, sorry. I'm in a bit of a muddle. I was having a nap.'

'I thought you were having a shower.'

'Oh, yes. I mean before... before I had a shower.'

In the small living room, Marconi sits down in the armchair close to the window.

Everything is very simple. Light colours, white sofa, white armchair, a small glass table and on it a photograph in a silver frame of the same girl smiling at someone with one of her sad smiles.

No pictures on the walls.

'Can I use *tu*?'

'Of course.'

'You can call me *tu* as well, like we did the first time. I have to ask you a few questions about your dream, the one you told me about the other week.'

Ten days of wanting to call her.

'Go on.'

'Can you describe the room in more detail? The one covered in blood, I mean.'

'Well... I'll have to think, it was a while ago now.'

'That's OK.'

Marconi looks at his hands, one of the few things he likes about himself, his hands. Strong hands, well kept, nice nails.

'It was white, narrow.'

'Anything else?'

'I don't know. I was staring at all that blood...'

'And the eyes?'

'Staring, frightening. It's happened, hasn't it? Something awful's happened?'

'Don't worry, nothing serious.'

If you can consider a pot-bellied man being butchered in the filthy toilet of a motorway café as nothing serious.

Viola feels nervous.

'Can I show you a photo?'

'Yes,' she says, though she would rather have said no.

He comes closer and takes the photographs out of his jacket pocket.

He bends down by her feet.

He shows her the photograph.

She lets out a cry and turns her face away.

In that same moment there is the sound of a key turning and the door opening.

Footsteps echoing.

'Who the fuck are you?' demands the man aggressively.

'Inspector Marconi. With whom do I have the pleasure of speaking?'

'Marco, Viola's fiancé.'

'Marco what?'

'Marco Di Giacomo. Why are you here?'

'Nothing special – it's for the INPS – the registered square footage of the flat is wrong.'

'But that isn't a job for the police, is it? And anyway, what the fuck does it matter, I've got the architectural plans.'

'All sorted – there was just a mistake somewhere. I'll be going now.' Marconi gets up. He shakes Marco's hand energetically, looking him in the eyes.

He receives an equally energetic handshake, and a fleeting look from eyes that are too dark and that move away immediately to rest on something else.

He's back in the corridor. The door closes behind him. Yet again, he has no idea what's going on.

It's almost dark. The inspector walks home, looking around him as he passes through the old area where the flower sellers are, near San Petronio.

He likes this street because it is narrow and full of flowers. There are flowers in pots, but he doesn't pay much attention to those: they're like domesticated animals. And then the cut flowers arranged in large bunches, or in coloured buckets standing on the ground.

They are depressing, cut flowers, because they already have death attached to them. They can't last very long; like fish on land.

Walking down that street always makes him think of death, but he likes that, since it makes him feel alive.

He walks along and looks at the flowers, and at the same time thinks about her, about the woman who holds him in the palm of her hand as she talks to him through her crimes, utterly brutal yet drenched in femininity.

In the end it turned out that she had left a little present the last time as well. After a few hours, the flying squad officers had gone back to check the scene of the crime again and found it.

A red rose, leaning up against an old scooter without any wheels.

Perhaps she had thought the scene of the crime wasn't complete, and so she went back to add the finishing touch.

A woman.

And like all women, she thinks details are important. Details, things that make a difference, and that men often undervalue.

He pictures her like that: a red rose with a cut stem. The queen of flowers; a determined woman looking for revenge.

It has just stopped raining. The smells are stronger. The stone of the city gives off a pungent fragrance. The perfume of the past, of ancient, timeless stories – the story of a victim and a murderer. But who is the real victim?

CHAPTER 37

The fridge is empty, as always.

He runs down the stairs and orders the usual Chinese takeaway from the place downstairs: Cantonese rice and spicy prawns.

He pays five hundred Euros a month in rent for a shoebox that constantly stinks of grease and yet he still eats it, that fried food.

Supper by the light of the street lamps, sitting in the armchair by the window. He likes to eat in the semi-darkness, without laying the table, while sipping a beer. There's always beer in the house.

Then he has a steaming hot shower. It's one of the few pleasures he allows himself every day.

He hasn't shaved for a week. His beard is now tough. He always means to wait for the shaving foam to soften it so as not to risk cutting himself, but he never does. Just takes time to rinse his hands, then shave and, every time, he cuts himself. As he does now.

Hanging on the wall is an old theatre bill. He found

it once in an attic when he was carrying out a search, and he took it away with him. It was left there, covered in dust, dating from 1976, with yellowing marks from the Sellotape and one corner almost torn off. *Brutal Justice*. What a film.

What a film, fuck, and then the ending – it was wild!

He remembers when he saw it the first time. He was just a boy. Sitting on the sofa, his feet didn't touch the ground. He was being good, sitting quietly and watching the television. It was Sunday afternoon and he had been swallowed up by the television screen as he watched a car chase. But what a car chase! Filmed with that workman like, high-speed shooting that cut across curves like the sharp scalpel of a surgeon.

He had leant to the right or the left, according to the bends, almost as if he himself were part of the chase.

He was on the side of the police. He was a cool guy, that Merli, with icy, fearless eyes; rough methods. One of those who see that justice is truly done.

And then the grand finale, when everyone might lose everything. Just one mistake, and it would all be over.

He has often watched that film again, but whenever he thinks about it, he only remembers that first time, on that Sunday afternoon when he decided that he would be like that, like the blond policeman with the moustache, without fear and without pity.

He does feel fear, however. He tried to grow a moustache but it didn't really suit his face, and as for pity... he doesn't exactly know what it is, pity. Occasionally he feels a tightening in his chest, but he doesn't know if you can call that pity. The only thing he is sure of is that when he sees certain things he feels an anger growing inside him, and if he got hold of...

The intercom sounds. It's Tommasi; he is waiting for him downstairs. Marconi dries his face and splashes on aftershave. It stings, making him wince.

'Inspector, you're bleeding – just under your ear.'

'I know, Tommasi, I know. I'll fit in better that way this evening. Don't they all think they're vampires in the club we're going to?'

Jokes have never been his strong point, and he knows it.

CHAPTER 38

Viola stands naked in front of the mirror. She scrutinises herself, something she hasn't done for ages.

She wants to prove to herself that she isn't hideous. She has hidden the jumper at the back of the wardrobe. She knows she is weak, having not thrown it away, which is what she would have liked to do in a rare burst of confidence. In moments of despair, she might need it again.

Yes, much better not to throw it away. And, anyway, she's hidden it so well that she can't see it. It's as if it never existed, she tells herself.

She stands on tiptoe on the tracksuit trousers she let fall to the ground a second ago.

She touches her thighs, almost as if she wants to view herself through touch as well. She slides her cold hands over her hips and up to her soft, firm, full breasts.

Her breasts. They seem so unashamed. If only she

were a bit more like them. She wishes she were erect like her nipples, taking on the world without fear. But she isn't a bit like her breasts, and so, to punish them and make them at least a bit like herself, she confines them in minimiser bras, trying to squash them, to flatten them.

Today, however, she wants to be more like them.

On a chair next to her is everything she needs. The black lace slip that usually she feels embarrassed about wearing. She puts it on, and the shiny material bunches up around her breasts, struggling to get past them but then sliding down and barely concealing her behind a veil of seduction.

It's as if she is dressed in a sensual spider's web, and for an instant she thinks she looks beautiful. She considers that she ought to put on a bra, but then dismisses that idea, remembering those words of his that hurt her so much.

No, she isn't like that jumper.

She picks up the stockings. They're new. She went to the supermarket and found a nice black pair. She didn't even know that they sold them in the supermarket, stockings like this. She runs into the bathroom and puts her old clothes into the washing basket, then fetches her mascara and pink eyeshadow. She lengthens her eyelashes and makes them thicker and sexier, then colours her eyelids with a subtle touch of powder.

She holds her face further away from the mirror. There's something missing. Lip gloss. She has to sparkle.

She goes back to the large mirror and is admiring her reflection when the door opens. She jumps. She would have liked to study herself for another few minutes. Instead, she dashes to the sofa and reclines on it like a diva.

She is a diva, not a shapeless jumper.

CHAPTER 39

There's a door policy. The bouncer looks them up and down for a second and then lets them in, even if they don't really fit in with the kids with extended fangs or the girl with white contact lenses in the queue alongside them.

Marconi stared at him with a face that meant trouble, and the bouncer recognised the look. A cop.

'Don't pull out your badge unless you need to. We're just here to have a look round. She was probably here last week and I don't think she would have gone unnoticed, so keep your eyes open and try to question the right people,' the inspector says to Tommasi, who is already eyeing up the arse of a girl in a miniskirt so short he can see her knickers.

Marconi looks round. It's early; the dance floor is as empty as a church on Saturday afternoon.

He tries to spot the locals, the regulars.

He decides to visit the washroom.

There's a large, fat guy with an earful of earrings. A

silver-coloured chain links the last of them to a large ring inserted in his bottom lip. He's peeing, leaning against the urinal.

Marconi moves closer, undoes his fly and tries to pee.

'Hey, man, do you come here often?' Out of habit he looks at the man's hands, noticing a large tattoo that goes from his index finger right up to his elbow.

The man shakes off the last drops with two sharp movements, does up his fly and crosses his arms in front of his chest.

'Go and talk to someone else, you piece of shit. You're lucky you're peeing and I don't want to get my boots dirty. But get in my face again and you're fucked,' and he swipes his hand across the front of his throat in an unambiguous gesture.

Marconi, visibly uneasy, creeps out of the bathroom and goes to sit down on a sofa.

There's a girl sitting opposite him.

Ugly, really ugly.

Aquiline nose, thin lips. *Too* thin. Wearing a black outfit with bits of material hanging off it, looking like something that has come back from the dead.

He smiles at her. She lowers her eyes.

No one pays any attention to her. This is my chance, he thinks, still with a healthy dose of optimism.

'What's your name?' And he smiles at her.

'Shadow.' She holds out her hand. She has enclosed her fingers in gloves made out of fishnet stockings. They stretch above her elbows.

'Shadow?' he repeats.

She opens her eyes wide.

She's definitely asking herself what planet I'm from.

'Are you enjoying yourself?'

'I never enjoy myself.'

'Oh.'

An embarrassing silence.

'Nice outfit, with all those... bandages.'

'Are you taking the mickey?'

She gets up and goes.

Ugly and a yob. Marconi adjusts his black shirt – like the one he wore to his uncle Luigino's funeral. His mother had bought it specially for the occasion.

That was a memorable day, the first time he had seen a dead person.

Everyone said: 'How beautiful and serene he looks, like he's sleeping.' But he himself hadn't been able to look at uncle Luigino for more than ten seconds, it upset him so much.

He used to see him every Christmas, at lunch with his relatives. A stout man, always cheerful. Not that shrunken thing that looked like the mummy he had seen in a history book.

'Look at him, son,' Aunt Santina had said to him. 'We all end up like that.'

When he swallowed, his saliva felt like a piece of cement. It had made a noise going down.

People are ugly when they die, he had thought.

Marconi goes over to the bar. He decides to have a drink and try to loosen up a bit.

He looks around again. The dance floor is still half empty. No one attracts his attention: just people in their weird outfits, and the large man from the washroom who is pointing at him as he talks to his friends.

Fuck.

He hurriedly turns round.

He orders a Southern Comfort and leaves a tip for the barman, ring in his nose and a black satin shirt artfully left open to show off his nipple piercing.

'So, your job must be hard... always being polite, serving people all night. And then, younger people are always the worst, always more bad-mannered, don't you think?' Marconi knows how much survivors of the Eighties enjoy running down the younger generation.

'Tell me about it! But every now and then you meet nice people,' and the barman smiles at Marconi.

'What are people like here?'

'Always the same faces. The goths act a bit superior and don't try to make friends. You're new here, aren't you?'

'Yes, but then you must know everyone!'

'I've worked here for two years. As I said, it's always the same people.'

'A friend told me about this place – she's new too,' hazards Marconi. 'She came last Friday but I'm sure you won't have seen her; you can't expect to notice everyone,' and he takes a sip of his drink.

'Of course, I did – the blonde, the femme fatale.'

Marconi plants himself down on the bar stool.

'Very fashionable, pale skin, red lips – a stunning girl. She isn't your girlfriend, is she?'

'No, no. As if! She's just a friend,' and he immediately regrets having said 'As if'.

'I wasn't the only one who noticed her. As soon as someone new arrives, they're all like vultures.'

'And you?'

'Oh, definitely not me.'

'So, what makes you sit up and take notice?' Marconi is trying to be friendly, in order to get as much information as possible out of him.

'Eyes turn me on. Eyes like bottomless pools, that cut you in two if you're not ready for them. Like yours.' The barman gives him a mischievous look.

'Thanks. Yours aren't bad either.' He feels embarrassed, then adds, 'I imagine she was busy trying to seduce someone.'

'Who?'

'My friend, last week. I'll tease her about it when I get home.'

'Ah, but then it's true that she's your girlfriend,' and the bartender turns his back on him.

Marconi looks round to check that there's no one nearby. The tattooed man is right behind him.

He would like to be able to disappear, but he has to know more.

'I told you she's not my girlfriend. She's just a friend. We share a flat with two other people. You know, it's hard to pay the rent when you're a student,' Marconi adds, talking slightly more quietly.

'What? I can't hear you if you whisper.'

'I don't have a girlfriend.'

The barman turns to him, smiling.

'Hey, faggot, we're thirsty here.'

I'll turn round suddenly, grab his head and slam it down on the bar. I'll show him my badge, shouting: 'Police, you bastard!'

Instead, Marconi stays where he is, being chatted up by the camp barman.

'Here's your Jack Daniels, but you don't have to be so rude.' The barman puts down a round glass strategically filled with a generous shot of golden liquid, enough to keep the lout away from them for a while.

'Where were we? Don't pay any attention to him. I've known him for years, and he's like that, but he's not dangerous.'

'Good. So, tell me, I'm curious, did my friend do anything she shouldn't, last Friday?'

'You really are nosy, aren't you? OK, I'll satisfy your curiosity. But only if you let me buy you a drink.'

'OK,' is all Marconi manages to say, swallowing the last mouthful of his Southern Comfort. 'Well? But tell me everything, OK?'

'OK, I'll tell you. She danced a bit and then…'

'And then?'

'What do I get if I tell you?'

'Tell me first and then we'll see.'

'You're a tough guy, eh?'

Fuck. Are you going to tell me or do I have to rip it out of you? Marconi thinks, but all he says is 'Go on.'

'She danced for a bit, but from about halfway through the evening she then stopped being competition for me.' He puts his hand over his mouth to hold back a snigger.

'How do you mean?'

'Are you jealous?'

'I am not jealous,' Marconi says slowly. He's losing his patience.

'She picked up another girl and they put on a show on the sofa there at the back. Those poor disappointed little boys.'

'So she disappointed a lot of people.'

'Well, yes. But now let's talk about you. You must need a licence for a mouth that sexy...' He pours him another drink.

Marconi thinks about getting out of there, but just at that moment the barman points at a girl and says: 'There, that girl over there. She's the one she was with, the girl with long hair. Samantha, she's called. Spelled the English way, of course. She used to go out with the DJ, then he dumped her and now she gives it away to anyone who wants it... men, women and small animals.' He laughs.

Marconi picks up the whisky the barman has just put down on the counter and turns his back on him, leaving him looking puzzled.

'You're so rude! Where are you going?' the barman shouts at Marconi's back, then he turns away angrily.

Tommasi has disappeared.

It's her. I bet it's her. I can feel it.

The dark-haired girl that the barman has just pointed out is sheathed in a long dress made of some glossy fabric. She has started to dance in the middle of the dance floor, which is now filling up, her eyes half closed and her lips soft. She is amazingly sensual.

Marconi, who can't dance and feels ill at ease, moves towards her and improvises.

'I need to talk to you. It's important.'

She doesn't answer and carries on dancing.

'They told me that last week you were with my girlfriend. I need some sort of explanation,' he adds seriously.

'Who do you think you are?' she replies sullenly.

'Listen. I know it's nothing to do with you, but I hope you can understand.'

The girl turns her back on him, and a few people at the side of the dance floor start to stare at him rudely.

Marconi tries playing the melodrama card. They say it works, with women. 'I'm totally in love with her,' he says in his best soap-opera voice, looking down at his feet. 'Marta and me have been together three years, but she cheats on me every time she goes out. I know she does, but I can't leave her. And no one has the courage to tell me the whole truth about what she gets up to.' Then he pretends he's walking away.

'Wait,' he hears behind him. 'OK, sit down,' she says, suddenly sympathetic.

She leads him towards a mirrored corner where a large velvet armchair invites people to escape from the crowds of people.

'My boyfriend used to cheat on me too, and he didn't waste any time in dumping me, that shit. But what did you want to know?'

'I'd like to know how far she went. Did you just kiss?'

'We danced. We eyed each other up, as you do, then she moved towards me and started to brush against me. I took her by the hand and... but I didn't know she was spoken for.'

'Don't worry about it. You couldn't have known. But what else did she do?'

'We sat down – here, in fact. This is my favourite spot because it's so intimate – and we started kissing. She kisses really well, but you'd know that better than me. Things warmed up a bit... I'm not exactly an iceberg. And when she started to bite my neck, I whispered to her to follow me. We went into the bathroom... and it'd be better if I didn't tell you anything else.'

Marconi struggles to hide his own arousal. He realises that he's as hard as those other men before they died. That isn't a reassuring thought. He tries to cover the fact by taking off his scarf – because of the heat – and draping it across his lap.

'No, carry on.' He ought to press her to reveal details about what the suspect looks like, rather than about their sexual activity in the loos.

The girl, who doesn't seem to need any encouragement, takes his hand in a gesture of support and rests it on her thigh, which is left uncovered by the split in her skirt. Just at that moment the tattooed man walks past.

He is definitely a biker.

Marconi tries to hide by lowering his head between his hands.

'Samantha, just forget about him. He's got different tastes.' The man then bursts out laughing. 'He likes dogs, not cats.' And he laughs again. 'He doesn't play football, he prefers a bat.' He sounds like he could go on forever.

Marconi's erection has gone. And he breathes a sigh of relief as he hears the laughter from that heavily built, leather-clad jerk moving away. One problem solved.

She starts talking again, her eyes fixed on his. She articulates every word clearly, omitting not a single detail. She explains how she pushed the other girl gently against the pink wall of the bathroom, how she lifted her dress and slipped off her black panties. And she talks; she talks on without ever breaking eye contact with Marconi. Every pause leaves him hanging on those full, seductive lips, and the story they are relating.

He feels aroused a second time, burning with desire. He is aware that he is gripping her hand, and he forces himself to speak in an attempt to shatter the spell of her story.

'Thanks. You don't know what you've done for me,' he says, slightly hesitant, rearranging his scarf. 'You know, I gave her that dress for her birthday,' he then adds, like an accomplished actor.

'You've got great taste. I love oriental-style dresses, and black and red are my favourite colours. If I were her, I wouldn't let a man like you get away. I'll tell you a secret: the touch of satin drives me wild,' she says, as if trying to recreate the magic of a moment before.

'How naïve I was to fall in love with someone like her. It was her eyes that struck me the first time I met her in Piazza Maggiore. I was sitting in Neptune's shadow, when she walked by and glanced over.'

'Yes, I know that look. Two crystal-blue eyes that seem to see right inside you.'

'And you? You'll think I'm a masochist, but I'd like to know what it was about her that attracted you.'

The girl briefly closes her eyes as if to conjure up an image.

'Her blonde hair against that pale skin, the full mouth... I liked everything about her, including that fantastic hairpin of hers. Imagine, she wouldn't even let me touch it. It must be very important to her.'

'I don't think I've ever seen it.'

'Come on, you must remember it, it's so beautiful. It's like a ceremonial dagger, inlaid with two red stones at the end.'

Marconi's eyes light up.

'A dagger?'

'I couldn't think of a better word. It was a type of metal hairpin. Don't tell me you can't remember it. I once saw something similar at Montagnola, but it couldn't even compare with hers.'

'Who knows who gave it to her. But, you know what I say? After this evening, it's not my business any more.'

With that hairpin she probably skewered a human eyeball.

'Let's have some fun. What did she tell you her name was?' he then asks her, holding his breath.

'She didn't tell me anything about herself. You know, we didn't talk very much... But I want to give you a piece of advice: why don't you get your own back? You'll feel much better.' She watches him languidly.

He reckons that it has been too long since he last had sex. A good fuck, not like the one with Sabrina that evening. But then he controls himself and declares that he'll have to finish with his girlfriend first. He can't wait. He gets up and leaves her sitting there, slightly stunned, on the red velvet sofa.

CHAPTER 40

Make-up smeared on her eyes – a mess, like the bed she is stretched out on. A dishevelled doll: naked, fucked and abandoned. He has gone out again this evening. He didn't say much. 'You're beautiful, but what have you done? You don't even look like "you".'

Why not? What is 'me'?

Why can't this girl be me, and the girl in a tracksuit and no make-up only a version of me that I put on like a disguise every so often? Why not?

Who decided what I am? How have I ended up like this? Imprisoned in a character I don't particularly like.

Yes, I hate myself.

Because of my insecurity, because of my fear. Yet I can't change. This is how I am.

The slip is now just a heap of fabric lying by the end of the bed. It has stopped being an instrument of seduction. She hugs her teddy bear and seeks out the flesh under her fingernails.

When I taste the sweetness of my blood, I'll stop. I don't want to dream tonight. I just want to see darkness.

Darkness that swallows her up.

She lies still and breathes deeply. She thinks about how he made love to her.

He put himself inside me by just pulling my knickers to one side. He didn't even take them off. He felt heavy on top of me, burning me inside.

He stung, like his coarse stubble. He smelled like he always smells before he has a shower. It was over quickly, too quickly for the pain to turn to pleasure. But do women ever enjoy sex?

In the magazines they say they can, but I don't believe it.

It's a lie. One of the many lies they write. Like 'surprise him and he'll be yours forever' or 'conquer him in the kitchen' or 'pretend you don't care and he won't be able to resist you'.

If he comes home and I pretend I don't care, he'll go out again in five minutes. It's complete rubbish. And I'm an idiot to fall for it.

She has smeared on her face the moisturiser they said would give her perfect skin. She spent twenty-five Euros on it and her skin is still red. On the cold floor, there's a lace slip that isn't a lace slip any more: it's just a shapeless piece of material.

As soon as he finished he went to wash my smell from his body. And he shaved.

I still smell of him, yet I'm here alone.

CHAPTER 41

'I need to see Mariangela,' Eva says, sounding serious.
'She's busy. You can speak to me.'

'Roberto, I need to speak to Mariangela. If I'd needed to speak to you, I would have said so.'

'At this precise moment, you should be busy at the scanner, getting those images ready which I asked you for,' he replies, annoyed.

'The sooner I speak to Mariangela the sooner you'll have your scans.'

'Well! Listen to that determination!' he jeers at her.

'Enter,' says the voice behind the frosted-glass door.

The girl goes in and stands by the desk.

'What is it, Eva, that's so important you need to interrupt me in what I'm doing?' asks the woman, somewhere between surprise and annoyance.

'Mariangela, you know I respect you, but I've worked here for two years now and no one's given me a chance to show what I can do. Obviously, I don't want you to hand over a publicity campaign to me on trust – I just want a chance.'

'You know it's Sonia and Roberto who –'

'Sorry to interrupt, only I don't want to waste your time. I've had another job offer – from a competitor, I mean. If you're not going to give me a chance to get more involved, I'll have to accept it. All I'm asking is for you to give me a try.'

'A try in what sense?'

'The new campaign for mobile phones. I'd like to be able to present my ideas as well, and then the client can decide. If they choose Sonia or Roberto that's fine, but I'd like to be considered a bit more from now on.'

'OK, but this mustn't take you away from the other things you're supposed to do.'

'You can take that for granted. Thank you for having faith in me.'

'Now, off you go. And shut the door behind you,' says Mariangela, reminding her who's in charge.

There, she has given herself a birthday present; she has persuaded Mariangela to give her a chance. She knows that from now on the woman will make her pay dearly for it, but that doesn't matter; she now has her chance.

Roberto gives her a surly look as she comes out of the boss's office, walking unusually tall.

The day seems lighter to her now. Like the first few months of working there, when she used to complete her tasks quickly, full of hope, dreaming that soon she would see her own adverts around town, and she would be able to stop and stare at them, with her nose in the air and her heart smiling.

Leaving work, Giulia, as usual, talks non-stop while they walk to her birthday surprise.

'We're here. Come on. I know you don't drink much, but I'll buy you one anyway – the barman's great – and then you can open your present.' Giulia has a voice like honey, the one she uses when she wants to be sure of getting *yes* as an answer.

The bar is near the Two Towers, rather hidden, but it must be fashionable because it's full of young people. They're crowding around outside as well, making a racket.

Good, it's really close to the bookshop, thinks Eva, *so I'll be able to go and have a wander round it afterwards.*

They go in. It's very bright, with African paintings on the walls and ebony statues dotted here and there. The barman really is cute: short hair, serious, and he doesn't look like he puts on airs, which in itself is extremely unusual.

'What can I get for you?'

'Two glasses of white wine. It's my friend's birthday,' Giulia chirps to attract his attention.

'Congratulations! I'll get you some special nibbles as well then.'

'I melt when he speaks. Have you ever seen such a hunk? God, I'll dream about him tonight.'

'You could stop telling everyone it's my birthday,' Eva says.

'Come on, don't be your usual sulky self. Life smiles on those who smile at it... or something like that.'

Giulia is always in a good mood when she can spot a new conquest on the horizon. She likes to find a fresh object of desire fairly frequently: once she gets what she wants, she has already lost interest in it, and is looking for something new. She is in a permanent state of euphoric non-happiness.

'Here we are,' says the barman. 'The sandwich with the little coloured flag is for the birthday girl. It's got a special filling, with a dressing I invented myself.'

'Thank you.' Eva feels embarrassed.

'Don't be a flirt. Hands off – I saw him first,' Giulia says, pretending to be joking. She hands her the shiny black parcel that she has been holding and exclaims 'Happy birthday.' Everyone turns to look at Giulia and she covers her mouth to pretend she didn't reveal it on purpose, that it just slipped out. She's always over the top.

'But you shouldn't have,' Eva tells her.

'At least open it, then you can say I shouldn't have.'

The birthday girl scratches off the Sellotape with her fingers. She does it carefully; the paper is so nice that she doesn't want to spoil it. It's like the wrappers of those toffees in the fuchsia tin with the picture of a lady and a cavalry officer on the lid, the sweets her grandmother used to give her every Christmas when she was a girl. The lady held a lace parasol and wore a bonnet. Eva can still remember her as if she had the tin in front of her. How soft and sweet they were, those toffees. They used to melt in her mouth... Her favourites were the long, thin caramels.

'Come on! You're taking ages!'

'OK.' Eva tears off the paper and reveals a white cardboard box. She waits a second before raising the lid, just like when she was small and paused before unwrapping her favourite caramels. Then she gives in to curiosity and lifts the lid abruptly.

A dress – a dress the like of which she has never seen before.

'But were you all in on this together?' she says, thinking of her sister's present.

'So, you like it, then? I bought one the same for me. Just so I'm not jealous of any of my friends, I've learned a trick: if I buy them a present, I buy one for me as well. That way there's no problem.'

'Thank you. It's stunning,' Eva says, even though she doesn't think she'll ever wear it. She plays with the flag from the sandwich, twisting it between her fingers.

'Promise you'll wear it.'

'I don't know, but it really is beautiful, Giulia.'

It's as if the whole world is telling her that she's a woman, and she can't hide the fact any longer. Her periods, which have been starting early for a while now, perhaps even they want to remind her. Tell her that she should stop pretending that all she needs is a pair of jeans, heavy combat boots and a hood pulled over her head to hide her from the world.

A world that seems to her to resemble a huge cock. A world that, as far as she can see, isn't the shape it ought to be. It's not round any more, it's a big cock.

The dark keeps her company as she goes home. She looks down at her feet, as usual, concentrating on the scuffed toes of her shoes. She has bought a book. The heroine is a woman detective; the story is set in Bologna.

Today I got lots of presents. She keeps her gaze on her shoes, racing along quickly to carry her home – to her Miew.

She has just turned the corner of Via dell'Inferno when a dodgy-looking figure suddenly appears.

He has a red scarf wrapped tightly round his neck and is clutching something in his hand. For an instant Eva feels as strong as an ox. The blood is pounding in her temples like a hammer, and a strange heat spreads throughout her body.

CHAPTER 42

'Hello?'
                    'It's me.'
'Who's speaking?'
'Viola. Sorry to disturb you.'
'Oh. Hi Viola. No, you're not disturbing me.'
'Thank you for the other day. It probably seemed odd but I didn't want my boyfriend to know...'
'I understand. It's not a problem.'
'Is someone dead?'
'What?'
'The photograph, the blood.'
'Viola, I can't talk about this. Especially not like this, on the phone...'
'I understand. Listen, below my flat there's a café, and if you like we could meet there in half an hour.'
'Perfect.'

The girl wanders round the room in bare feet. The bad weather is almost over; it will soon be replaced by longer, sunnier days. She loves it when it's cold. For various reasons.

She pulls on a pink stretchy top and a pair of jeans. She has put on weight, a kilo. She can see it in her breasts – they're enormous.

She hates her tits. Too big. Far too big.

It's as if they call out to men, as if they say *look at me, I'm female*.

Female.

She doesn't even like the word.

It makes her think of sex.

It makes her think of people having sex.

Every day.

Having sex every day.

When it's her period, she doesn't like having sex, but... Marco tells her that he likes it, that she smells female when she bleeds. Female.

She hates that word.

She has always hated it.

She changes again. She puts the pink top back in the wardrobe; it's too tight. She opens the door of Marco's side of the wardrobe and takes out a black-and-green checked shirt.

There's not much time before their meeting. She is nervous.

Partly because she has had that dream again.

Roses bathed in blood. Cut roses. Death.

It's three o'clock on the dot. Perhaps he's already waiting for her.

She runs down the stairs. Marconi is sitting at a table. He feels relaxed and flirtatious – a rare occurrence, it doesn't happen often. He has ordered a coffee, no sugar.

'Hi,' she says, while still in the doorway.

157

'Hi.'

It feels like their first meeting.

'Do you want something to drink?'

'No thanks.'

'What did you want to tell me?'

'I've changed my mind – I'll have a *caffè macchiato*. With hot milk.'

'OK.' Marconi raises his arm to call the *barista*.

'There's no waiter service here.'

'What?'

'You have to go to the counter. Better still, I'll go.'

'No, wait, I didn't understand. I'll go.'

Viola looks out of the window. She smells Marco's domineering odour on the shirt. She hugs herself, clasping her hands round her arms and imagining that she is touching him. There is something in the pocket over her breast. She reaches in and feels something smooth.

'Here's your coffee, miss.' Marconi bows to her like a waiter. He's in a good mood, which he hardly ever is. 'It's hot today, isn't it?' he adds, sitting down again.

'Yes, too hot – and it's only the end of March.'

'I like the heat.'

'The eyes are the same.'

'What?'

'The eyes in the photograph. They're the same as in my dream.'

'I thought so, from how you reacted the other day.'

'They looked like they belonged to a person in my dream, but instead it's just a soft toy. Only a soft toy. Such a lot of fear for a teddy bear.'

'Well, yes.'

'You don't know what a weight you've lifted from me. I mean, I'd much rather it was a teddy bear. I recognised the floor as well, and the toilet in the background. Now I understand what it was. It was a toilet.'

'But what is it you do with your life?' And he smiles at her with his eyes.

'I survive, not much more than that,' and she smiles, too. Then she passes her hand over the pocket and hears whatever it is crunching. She can't wait any longer. She has found something. Perhaps a note from another woman. Perhaps she won't be able to pretend any longer that nothing's wrong. She tries to work out what it is, feeling the shirt pocket with her hand.

Marconi watches her. *She looks sad.*

'I'd like to get a job.'

'They always need shop assistants in town. Have you tried to find anything?'

'Not yet. I'm slow in just making a decision, so imagine how long it takes me to actually do something.'

'So… he's your boyfriend?'

'Yes.' They stop talking. He plays with the teaspoon. She keeps feeling the pocket to work out what is hidden inside.

'OK. I have to go now.'

'Can I walk with you?'

'Better not.' She says goodbye to him so she can be alone with whatever it is that's inside the pocket.

CHAPTER 43

'Today's the big day,' says Roberto, ironically.

He has no doubt about it: he's going to humiliate her again. And he'll punish her as well, for not staying in her place like he said she should.

He also feels sure because the client is a friend of Mariangela's husband, and because of that he always listens to her advice. Therefore, even if Eva produces something halfway decent... but then she isn't any good. There's no doubt about that either. All she's capable of is doing the scanning.

'Eva, they're waiting for us in the presentation room. The client is already here,' he informs her while he adjusts one of his awful ties, this one in shades of acid green.

The girl sits down, frowning, at one end of the long table of light-coloured wood.

Roberto is next to her, with a slight, affected smile on his lips. She hates him when he smiles like that, with his thin lips.

People whose lips are too thin are wicked, her grandmother always used to say to her.

There are two folders: her yellow one and Roberto's green one. She's sure it's just a coincidence, but she can't help noticing how it matches his tie.

Sonia is working on another project. At the last second they palmed off on her a newspaper ad promoting a beauty salon, partly because Roberto doesn't like having too many people under his feet when he wants to win over an important account.

Mariangela picks up the yellow folder and looks through it along with the client, a man of about fifty with a red face and a shiny nose, thin brown hair and a white-and-blue striped tie. She is speaking intently and he is nodding.

Then she takes the other proposal and starts talking to him quietly once more. The client nods again. 'I prefer the second one,' the man finally says.

Mariangela smiles, pulling back her lips until she is grimacing like a porn star. Perhaps she's thinking about the bonus she's now going to give Roberto, who is overjoyed about winning. An extra fuck.

'I'm sorry for Eva. She's new, and to build up her confidence I wanted her to have this opportunity, but there's no comparison is there, Guidetti? The second is much more immediate, more colourful, funny, right for young people and for the next Christmas campaign,' she concludes, articulating her words clearly.

'You have a look too, Giulia, seeing as you're here.'

Giulia doesn't even pretend to look at the two proposals and immediately says: 'The second one's much better. On a different level altogether. That girl in the Jacuzzi talking on her mobile is completely wrong.'

At that, Roberto's expression darkens. He jumps imperceptibly in his chair, and, unable to stop himself, fixes Eva with a stare that is somewhere between questioning and threatening.

She turns away while he thinks: *Don't say anything, just don't.* But she does.

'There must have been a mistake when the proposals were labelled. Look for yourselves: on the back of the design with the mobile phone snowboarding past the older models there's my signature. I don't know how it happened, but the two folders must have got mixed up. And now, as they say, give us youngsters a chance!'

Everyone looks at her – stunned – and she starts to talk to Guidetti, explaining her ideas in detail and the message she wanted to convey. No one can take it away from her now: the advertising campaign is hers. Soon she'll see her posters around Bologna, as she had dreamed, and every time she sees one she will imagine Roberto's face.

The shouting coming from Mariangela's office provides background noise during the last hour of the working day.

'That bitch. That fucking cunt. You shouldn't have let it happen!'

Then Mariangela speaks – no one can hear what she's saying – then Roberto again: 'Fuck. Fuck!'

Then nothing again.

'She swapped them, the bitch! I can't believe it. Fuck, I can't believe it.' Silence, then the sound of something crashing on to the floor.

Eva is enjoying it. She's loving every moment. A real orgasm of pleasure, like you get from chocolate, the same rush when you eat something that's so good you lick your lips and the taste fills you up and you try to stop it melting away.

Mariangela, however, won't be having any orgasms for a long time. He's very touchy is Roberto.

CHAPTER 44

'Tommasi, today's Friday and we're going to check out the market at Montagnola.'

'I thought the council did that sort of boring job.'

'We're trying to find the weapon used in the last murder, and we'll have a look round.'

'What? We're looking for an antique pistol at Montagnola?'

'No, I mean the hairpin used to spear the man's eye.' Marconi doesn't explain any further.

'OK,' is all Tommasi replies. Something crops up every time his boss says 'we'll have a look round', and they both know it.

Last time he said it, they found themselves in the middle of a shoot-out between a Ukrainian prostitute's pimp and a rather particular client: an ex-security guard who had got it into his head to take her off the street and marry her. They were there, just having a look round, in the area where the tobacco factory used to be. The shooting had started, and the woman – in a micro-skirt and high heels – was screaming. Her fingers were in her ears, and she was running backwards and forwards, unsure whether to side with her client or her pimp.

At Montagnola, Marconi makes sure he studies each and every stall, even though they all look much the same to him. And he doesn't like the smell of incense, either. It stings his nose and makes him sneeze. Tommasi follows a step behind, as it's so crowded that they can't walk side by side.

Every time Marconi halts, because he thinks he has just seen something that looks like a metal hairpin, without fail Tommasi bumps into him and says: 'Sorry, Inspector.' And Marconi replies, without fail: 'Don't call me inspector when we're undercover, you idiot.'

Sometimes they're just like a pair of comedians.

Marconi isn't very good at scanning the stalls – his eyes are too well trained in spotting criminality. He notices the actions of the Moroccan who is pretending to shake the rather dazed-looking Rastafarian's hand, but in fact is passing him a spliff. He sees the little punk who is walking too close to a boy with a rucksack, so he can open the zip a bit more every time the boy slows down. He would like to do something but then he remembers that it's not his business, that he's here to look for something very specific, something that perhaps will be able to provide some answers regarding the mysterious girl who goes round Bologna killing predatory men.

He is studying a stall that belongs to an Indian, where there are ebony hairpins decorated with perfect, tiny inlaid animals.

'Do you have any metal ones?'

'No, they look much nicer in wood, and they're more valuable.' The young man with hair so black and glossy it looks blue tries to persuade him to buy something.

'Do you know if anyone here sells metal hairpins?'

Just as he's asking the question, a girl shouts 'My bag!', and a gust of wind rushes past him like in a Roadrunner cartoon.

Marconi doesn't think; he just starts running, and slams into a short woman with curly hair who is admiring the faded top she has just bought. He roughly pushes her to one side. 'Sorry,' he shouts, and carries on racing after the thief who has now got further ahead of him.

Fifth year, the end-of-year sports day and by now struggling for breath. Antonio, repeating a year, and therefore two years older than him, was alone in front and sure of victory. Marconi had started to think that if he lost now, he would always lose in life, so he sped up, moving so fast that he caught and then overtook Antonio a few paces from the finishing line.

Keep trying. You can do it. And he thinks that it will be a bad omen – really bad – if he isn't able to catch the shit now running in front of him.

So he speeds up, trying not to lose sight of the orange fleece up ahead, trying to anticipate the movements of the people in his way so he can avoid them.

His spleen hurts. He pays no attention. He takes deeper breaths and carries on running. He runs and thinks that it will be a bad omen if he fails, and that he'll catch up like he did that time in the fifth year.

The boy turns a corner. Marconi speeds up. He can do this.

He skids round the corner, grabbing on to the wall for balance. The boy is nowhere to be seen. Marconi, all on his own, has just conjured up a mountain of bad omens for himself.

He stops. He struggles to breathe. His liver seems to have exploded inside him and his leg hurts.

Fuck me and my stupid superstitious games.

He notices that it is already starting to get dark, and there's still no sign of jewelled hairpins.

'Hi. What are *you* doing here?'

He straightens up and sees her. Boots up to her thighs, low-cut top and leather miniskirt, big earrings and eyes like a cat.

The girl from the club.

'Hi,' he manages to gasp, with difficulty.

'But what have you been up to?' she says. Her friends are watching him and burst out laughing.

'My dog,' he says, still panting.

'Your dog?'

Marconi hates it when someone repeats what he has just said, as if suggesting the most idiotic nonsense has just come out of his mouth.

'Yes.' He is still trying to get his breath back.

'So, are you going to tell me what happened to your dog, or do I have to worm it out of you?' Her friends all laugh again.

'I had him on his lead... he pulled on it... he ran off... I ran after him but... too fast.'

'You're worrying me gasping like that. Get your breath back!'

But can't those idiots do anything but laugh? And he gives them a severe look to make them be quiet.

Samantha is a step in front of them. She's the leader of the group, and it's clear that they all think she's the most beautiful.

'You don't know my good news. I've been really lucky... try and guess.' She pauses, then adds in a triumphant tone of voice: 'I found it!'

'What did you find?'

'What do you mean, *what*? A hairpin, just like your ex-girlfriend's – or at least I assume you've broken up with her by now.'

'Of course I have. But where? How did you find it?'

'There, right opposite. In a line of stalls parallel with Via Indipendenza there's Deco Mela, the craft market. A really sweet boy makes them. Look.'

She opens a yellow bag made of recycled paper and pulls out two hairpins, each one surmounted by two small glass spheres.

Marconi decides that women must possess a real skill, in being able to find what they're looking for among the chaos of all these stalls. Perhaps the bag snatcher wasn't such a bad omen after all.

'Can I?' he asks, holding out his hand.

'Take it,' she replies, suggestively.

It is about fifteen centimetres long, three millimetres in diameter, metal, therefore easy to sharpen. A little knife for the hair, in fact.

'It's lovely. It'll look really nice on you.' Marconi always feels slightly embarrassed around women.

She takes it from him, brushing her fingers against his hands, then asks him to wait a second before handing him a card on which she has already written 'Samantha' and a mobile phone number, with a little heart drawn after the last digit.

She kisses him on the cheek and starts to head off. 'Call me this evening and I'll let you know if I've found a poor old dog wandering all by himself round the city streets. You know, animals really like me. He'd happily follow me home.'

Shit, thinks Marconi as he goes to find his colleague. *But at least I know where to find the hairpins.*

CHAPTER 45

If he asks her anything, she'll deny it. But it's not as if he won't ask her anything, anyway. She is sure of that. She has put the shirt back in the wardrobe, but first she left it hanging on the door for a couple of hours and smelled it, occasionally.

She didn't think it still smelled of her, but Marco has an acute sense of smell, so she squirted some of his aftershave on it. Now it's in the wardrobe, exactly as before.

She has moved the packet it contained several times.

First she hid it in the new box of crackers. She made a small hole and pushed it in. Then she thought that Marco is often hungry when he gets home late at night, and he wouldn't bother finishing the old box of crackers before starting a new one. So she moved the packet to her wardrobe, stowing it in her underwear drawer. Under the white knickers, the ones she never wears, as she prefers black.

And what if Marco has brings a present – a new

pair of panties – and he goes to hide it with the others? So she moved the incriminating object again.

She fetched a chair and, standing on tiptoe, hid it on the top of the shelving unit in the living room. No, Marco once used to keep films up there, the banned ones, and she had discovered them. *Why didn't I remember that before?*

She put the chair back underneath, and she is standing there with the packet still in her hand. The door opens. She moves her hands as quickly as if what she's holding is red hot. She instinctively pulls at the waist of her trousers and slips it into her knickers.

'What are you doing, standing there in the middle of the room?'

'I was waiting for you.'

'Aren't you going to give me a kiss, then?'

Viola walks towards him. She can feel the packet between her legs.

'Is that all?'

'I've got a headache.'

'A headache. A woman's favourite excuse. What did you get up to today?'

'The usual.' She moves away from him.

'Good, good. Let's go and have a shower together.'

'I've just had one and, anyway, I told you I've got a headache. You go and have one.'

He comes closer. 'You know you're even more sexy when you have a headache?'

'I'll go and make dinner.'

Viola feels hounded. She hurries into the kitchen. After a minute he's there behind her. Her hands shake.

Marco turns her round and leans her back against the cold steel surface of the hob.

'No... really. I don't feel well.'

He starts to kiss her neck while she tries to wriggle free.

'No, not now. Leave me be.'

He pins down her hands so she can't move, and seeks out her mouth. Then he starts to caress her breasts. She is wearing a cotton T-shirt with long sleeves.

She is warm because of rushing around, while playing her game of pass the parcel. But now the game seems to have become a treasure hunt.

The packet. The fucking packet.

'Marco, no. I said no.'

He moves away for a second, then smiles. He is visibly aroused.

Why should something from that silly magazine prove to be true now? 'Say no and he'll take the first step.' Damn her pig-headed hope that some piece of their advice would turn out to be true. It serves her right.

He is pressing against her now, trying to pull her trousers down. He slides a hand between her warm thighs and keeps on kissing her face and throat.

'No.' She tries to get free of his grasp.

He turns her round as if she were an object. He pushes himself against her, her stomach pressing against the steel surface, which doesn't feel cold any more, and starts to move his fingers between her legs. 'Tell me you like it.'

He has never done this before. A hot, wet sensation, as if a piece of ice were suddenly melting. Her trousers and knickers have slid to her feet while his hand moves faster.

'No, stop it. Please.'

She doesn't have time to sense it coming. A strong, spontaneous orgasm that makes her shout out and arch her body backwards. She feels her legs give way. She falls to the floor, as he drops down on her so as to take his own share of pleasure.

Viola thinks about the packet that she just had time to slip into the coffee percolator. Then she reflects that orgasms really do exist. Those magazines aren't so silly after all.

CHAPTER 46

'How lovely. I've never seen such a beautifully laid table,' Eva says, enchanted. 'And the napkins! They're wonderful; they look like swans.'

'The maid does all this. My father only employs highly qualified staff.' Giulia assumes a superior tone of voice whenever she mentions their servants.

'But she's marvellous. What's her name?'

'Who?'

'The maid.' Eva strokes the swan-shaped napkin with the tip of her finger.

'How should I know? I just call her Giovanna. She's got one of those oriental names that you can't pronounce. We're in Italy so I call her an Italian name,' Giulia replies sharply.

'But are you celebrating something?' All this luxury has aroused Eva's curiosity.

'No, it's just a dinner for my father's business associates. Nothing out of the ordinary. I can't imagine what you'd say if you saw the table laid out for our New Year's Eve dinner! Last year there were Swarovski crystal snowmen to hold the place cards. Come on, I'll get changed, then we'll go to the gym. And then I'm seeing Andrea, so I'll have to take along something sexy to change into.'

Giulia starts to undress. She lets her clothes fall on the floor without taking her eyes from her reflection in the mirror. In bra and pants, she pirouettes on tiptoe while continuing to gaze at herself with a critical expression.

'I'll just be a minute, Giulia. I left my gym bag in the dining room,' Eva says, feeling bemused.

'Off you go, but be quick. We're already late, and you've still got to help me decide which outfit to take.'

Eva follows the long corridor which has its walls covered with paintings. There's one that always makes her feel uneasy: the portrait of a woman wearing a sullen look. The brush strokes convey a sadness that reaches out to the viewer, and Eva wishes she was able to speak to the woman in the painting.

'Why are you sad?' she asks, without waiting for a reply, as she then skips down the stairs, taking two at a time.

She goes into the dining room. The maid is arranging a centrepiece of flowers and exotic fruit.

'Sorry, it's only me.' Eva smiles. 'You're really clever, you know? Where did you learn to fold the napkins like that?'

'My mother taught me when I was a girl. It's a tradition in my country.'

'You really are good. I'm hopeless at doing things with my hands...'

She is a very young girl, not very tall, almond-shaped eyes and long, fine black hair bound in a plait.

'Thank you, miss.'

'Pleased to meet you. I'm Eva.'

'I'm Jin Holin,' and she bows. Eva does the same, before adding, 'I can't stay. If I don't go, Giulia –'

'Where have you been hiding. Come on, I'm ready.' Giulia mood has already altered. All it takes is for her to lose control over the people around her for a second and she becomes irritable.

'Sorry, I got lost.'

'Do you like my new tracksuit? I'm wearing something for my jazz class underneath – short and sexy. The tracksuit is just for getting to the gym.'

'It's lovely. Red suits you.'

'Of course. Everyone knows that blondes look good in red.'

'And the barman? Aren't you going to that bar near the Two Towers any more?'

'Oh, he's *old* news.' Giulia answers, clearly annoyed because he didn't pay her as much attention as she would have liked. 'I think he's gay,' she adds, to reassure her ego.

CHAPTER 47

What a shitty day.
A really shitty day.
But if he thinks he's going to cheat me out of my patch he's making a big mistake, that bastard.

He brought them up himself, those idiots: the first joints shared on the steps, the first highs. He had known them when they still had milk round their mouths and didn't even know how to roll a joint. He had had to roll the first one for them.

Who is it who puts himself out there to fix things for the clients? No one – except me. But why the fuck should I send them? It's not just that I've built up a personal relationship – which helps keep the clients grateful – but, as soon as they can, they'll try to fuck me over.

And then, when you think about when they started on the hard stuff – the phone calls at all hours, which was never enough... Always him to wipe their arses.

And now that shit, Fabietto, so sure of himself as leader of the gang that he's going to buy stuff direct from the Albanians and sell it back to the group. The shit they've got, those Albanians. But they're used to eating shit, those idiots. They wouldn't even recognise the good stuff from drugs that are cut again and again, they've been stoned for so long.

But if he thinks he's going to steal my business he's wrong.

I'll see to it that he never even thinks about that again.

He walks quickly while he talks to himself, with his mouth closed. The words are sitting on the tip of his tongue but all that escapes is an angry hiss from between clenched teeth.

He knows where to find Fabietto. He's moving quickly. He's almost there.

And then that fucking cop with the story about the INPS. But what do they think, that I'm stupid?

That I haven't worked out that something's going on? First at that whore's house and now at my own. They're even coming to my home. *The cops don't know how to do their job any more. They come to your home. Perhaps they even expect you to make them a cup of tea.*

He has arrived in Piazza Otto Agosto. He waits for a moment, with clenched fists, outside the arcade.

He goes in and sees him straight away. He has a plastic pistol in his hand and is shooting, leaning from side to side to dodge invisible bullets, and he's swearing.

He is almost on top of him. It's managed without any effort... *Fuck*, the bastard sees him, and doesn't even allow him time to realise that the boy has stopped shooting before he is already swerving round the other lads dressed in short bomber jackets with baseball caps on back to front.

He is leaving by the other door, his skateboard tightly in his hand. The doors are next to each other. Marco retraces his steps to try to cut him off.

'Out of my way, jerk!'

A thin boy with teeth missing holds up his arms as if to apologise.

Fuck!

He's already in the square and pushing himself off on his skateboard.

'Stop!'

Marco starts to run. It's Thursday morning and, in the square next to the entrance to the car park, there's a small group of stalls selling knick-knacks. Collectors and people clearing out their basements.

He slams his side into the corner of a wooden table.

'You little scoundrel!' An old man with a white beard shouts at him in dialect, before he bends over to pick up the military ribbons and medals of Mussolini that have been knocked to the ground.

The boy enters Via Maroncelli. Marco is gaining ground. Then he dives into Via Alessandrini, and in a second he's back in Via Irnerio. Marco's breath seems like smoke coming out of his mouth, because of the cold. He looks like a dragon. Perhaps he could finish him off with a burst of flame.

He's getting closer. He thinks he can smell the sour odour of sweat mixed with fear. The boy's heading towards a woman with a large basket full of cheap goods purchased from the discount shop at the end of the street. She's appeared from nowhere, and now she's in his way.

It's just like a videogame. People materialise –

zombies with staring eyes – and he has to avoid them. But it's as if he's reached an advanced level, where everything happens twice as fast. He instinctively swerves to the right, missing the woman but hurtling into a parked car.

The boy looks round and sees Marco just behind him. Marco is the monster at the end of the game, the boss that's hardest to kill. He turns his skateboard and hurls himself into the middle of the road. A car brakes and the driver swears.

Fabietto has passed to the next level. The monster is left standing with his mouth open, in front of the police car now stationary in the middle of the road.

Next to the driver, who is still cursing, the man from the INPS is staring straight at Marco through the lowered window.

Fuck!

Marco turns and starts to walk towards the portico.

Let's hope he didn't recognise me. What a shitty day.

'When a day starts like shit, it always ends like shit,' he says aloud, while he checks to see if the cops are leaving.

CHAPTER 48

She stares at the white ceiling. Last night she dreamed of red, everything was red. Like blood.

The first time she dreamed of red, the most blood she had seen up till then was when she scraped her knee outside her house. She fell as she got off her bicycle, because it was a bit too big for her. But she liked that because it made her feel more grown-up. She can't even remember how old she was.

It stung but she didn't cry. She just stared at it.

She looked at the grazed skin. She looked at the gravel that had gone into her knee, and that her mother then tried to extract with tweezers.

There was very little blood. But it was red: a colour that had somehow excited her.

Afterwards, she was left trembling slightly. Her mother thought it was because her daughter had had a scare, and made her a camomile tea with lots of honey.

She dreamed that very same night.

A road. And a pool of blood. She can see it there, in front of her, even now.

It wasn't red like the blood on her knee; it was more like a dense brown.

She woke up, crying out with fear.

For a long time her mother had stroked her forehead, which was damp with sweat, to make her go back to sleep. She sang softly, quietly – a story about a little girl who was too tiny to live in the world of adults, and who was always in danger of being trodden on.

'Poor baby, so tiny,' sang her mother, till in the end deep breathing took the place of her daughter's shallow and troubled gasps.

The day after that, they found the neighbour's dog.

Tom. He always ran free and played with all the children in the neighbourhood.

She had been holding on to her mother's leg and they were just going out; her mother was taking her to school. Then her mother yelled out her father's name, and at the same time pushed her daughter firmly back into the house.

From inside she could hear the neighbours shouting. At some point she ran outside.

What was left of Tom was a cascade of entrails falling from his ripped-open stomach, and soaked in his own blood.

For days she kept seeing that image. The real one, not the one from her dream. She couldn't understand it.

She just knew that it was the *same* image – and that it terrified her.

She stares at the whiteness of the ceiling. Last night she dreamed of red.

Blood. Blood everywhere. Staining everything.

Light.

And roses. Roses dipping their delicate petals in that sacred liquid.

It seemed to her that she could even smell it.

The sweetness of the blooming flowers. The sweetness of blood.

Together, in a macabre dance.

She hears a voice in her head calling her. All the time.

I can't bear it. Enough. A bit of peace. Please. Inside me.

She holds the packet of white powder between her fingers. It feels dangerous, as it always does when she holds it.

She has seen what you do in films. She must have seen it a thousand times.

In the end, it would be the only sure way of making everything disappear, that white powder.

It can't be difficult.

She pulls herself upright and stops staring at the ceiling above her. She moves her gaze from the white of the walls to the white of the packet. She puts it between her teeth and tears it open. She sniffs it. It stings her nostrils a bit and makes her eyes water for a moment.

On the coffee table in front of her is a straw that she has cut already.

She tips out a small pyramid of the powder. She makes a line. A snow-coloured snake slithering across the glass table-top.

I ought to think about this. But I need to feel silence

inside me. And I think it might help me. Then I'll burn it, the packet. I want to make it disappear.

She looks into the eyes of the snake. She moves the straw towards it, to tame it.

She sniffs hard.

CHAPTER 49

'Hi Patrick. How are you?'
   'Not great, Eva. Sorry.'
   'What's wrong?'
   'I know. To be polite I should say I'm fine, but the fact is I'm not fine,' the boy answers dismally, and lowers his gaze to his skinny knees.
   'But what's happened?' repeats Eva.
   'The usual. Nothing new.'
   'For me, it's insane at work. I'm the newest person there and everyone pulls my leg.'
   'Really?'
   'Yes, really. And, trust me, it does get to me. Some days I'd happily stay in bed.'
   'It's the same for me at school... but there's one guy in particular.'
   'There's always someone in particular who ruins your life. It's true for everyone.'
   'No, I don't believe it happens to everyone.'
   'Well, it's true for people like us, quiet people who

don't want to bother anyone, who just mind their own business.'

'Yes, it is like that. So why doesn't everyone else just live their own lives?'

'Because sometimes it's better to live other people's. It's easier.'

'Let's start now. No more chatting.'

A bit of running round the room. Jumping on the spot. Stretching.

Eva thinks about how it is true: someone takes the trouble to force their way into your life, and destroys it. Destroys the balance you have established.

Everything changes. Even the colour of your eyes. She's sure of that.

The colour of her own eyes has changed.

Press-ups.

It's like a vase that falls and breaks. You can stick it back together, but it's never quite the same as it was before.

Exercises in pairs.

Eva joins up with her friend.

She holds the cushion first. He hits it angrily.

He lacks co-ordination. She has to try to guess what he's going to do so she can cover herself and not be hit. He's like a missile without a target, putting too much force into his punches. Force without control is useless.

'Eva, at school, that person I was telling you about before...' And he throws a punch, but swings his arm out too wide. Any opponent would have time to land a direct hit and knock him flat before his hook connects. 'I don't mind when he insults me, but he insults someone I care for very much.'

186

'Patrick, punch straighter.'

'I can't stand it any more.'

'I know what you mean. But you have to have a bit of patience in this world...'

'I'd give anything to make him stop, when he starts insulting her the way he does.'

'Try to raise your leg a bit more when you kick.'

'I wish he'd never mention her again, my mother, never.' Another semicircle that loses its momentum before he even lands the punch.

'Change over!'

Patrick takes the cushion.

Eva puts the gloves on.

'You're right, Patrick. You can't do anything about it.'

He looks at her, downcast. Even his only friend is saying he can't do anything. And therefore he's not worth anything.

As Eva throws a right-hander, the force of the blow makes him step backwards.

'As a fellow student, you'd risk being expelled if you touched him, wouldn't you?'

The boy smiles, thinking for a second that what Eva is saying is true, that she didn't say it just to make him feel better, to boost his morale, but because he really could beat up Stefano if he wanted to, but he doesn't do so because he doesn't want to cause problems for himself.

'Listen, Patrick, what school do you go to?'

'That's enough chatting. What's up with you two today?' The coach stares over at them.

Eva does a high kick.

'Righi. Why?'

'Because…'

'Silence, there! Eva, right, you can train with Lara. Patrick with Luca. I'll have to split you up, like kids. Now, when I clap my hands you do a middle kick: one, two three. Now high kicks: one, two, three.'

Eva gets her anger off her chest. Every kick fills her with adrenalin, recharges her. She feels the force of her blows against the leather cushion, which the girl with plaits is struggling to hold on to, and tries to make them even more powerful and precise. The part of the lesson she likes best is towards the end: free fighting. That's when she has the opportunity to compete with a person, flesh and blood, not a stuffed sack, so she can't make any mistakes because, if she does, she risks being kicked or punched. And in those moments she gets the opportunity to challenge her own fear. To let herself get hurt.

She studies her opponent and doesn't ever consider that, when all's said and done, it's just a training exercise; she thinks the person in front of her wants to hurt her, and then her eyes change colour and she becomes a lioness.

'Eva, wait a minute.' The coach is looking serious.

Shit, here we go. He's going to tell me off.

'There's no sense in you staying with this course.'

'But… it won't happen again.'

'You've improved a lot. From next Tuesday come to the advanced course. I'll see you at eight instead of seven.'

CHAPTER 50

S he can't do it again.
  Too little time has passed. She has to be careful.
He could walk in on her at any moment.

But he won't.

Marco has gone out again, but there's something
else... He's not his usual self. They haven't made love
for days.

That's never happened before.

Perhaps it really is over between them.

She wanders backwards and forwards across the
room, unable to settle. She throws herself on to the
sofa and tries to find a bit of warmth by hugging a
cushion. She still feels cold, and she hears the voice.
The voice inside her.

Instinctively she brings her fingers to her mouth.
She tries to find a piece of fingernail. Biting her nails
would calm her down, but there's nothing to get hold
of. She looks at her hands. Her nails no longer exist.
They are just stumps that go straight into her flesh.
Her hands look horrible; she thinks they are hideous.

No wonder Marco won't touch me any more – I'm disgusting.

She studies her nails again and bursts into tears. She jumps to her feet and goes into the bathroom.

She fetches something, then comes back and sits down in the living room, this time on the chair standing in the corner.

She starts brushing nail polish on to what's left of her nails with their reddish edges. She cries as she skims the brush over them. She shouldn't bite them like that any more. This is the last time. Now they'll grow properly and she won't touch them again. Enough is enough. This time it's final. She won't bite them ever again. She still cries.

There is soon more polish on her skin than on her nails, but she thinks they already look much better.

Yesterday Marco ate quickly and had his shower straight after lunch. Usually he doesn't take a shower early in the afternoon. He has one in the evening before he goes out, or on Sunday if they have made love in the morning, to wash her smell off his skin.

Yesterday, Marco was behaving strangely. He didn't even notice that she had put on her black bangles again, the plastic ones. She has had them since she was a girl, when she was a Madonna fan. She used to think she looked so beautiful with her bangles. They went up almost to her elbow.

The made her feel good, and they hid everything.

Because even back then she was like she is now, but with Marco she had to stop, because he hasn't let her wear her bangles.

'They look like gaskets or something,' he would say, 'and I don't want you wearing them. I'll buy you gold ones once I'm rich.'

She needed to put her bangles on again, and he hasn't even noticed.

CHAPTER 51

The kids are spreading across the street like a multicoloured stain. They chatter and shout as they walk along under the weight of their rucksacks. Watching their behaviour, the way they move and communicate, you can tell which ones have already had a tough life – as well as those who never will, the bastards and the bimbos of tomorrow.

Patrick is hunched over, not looking at anyone. He walks quickly, as if he's trying to get away from something. Or someone.

That someone soon catches up with him.

'Hey, shit face. Hey, I'm talking to you. Turn round.'

Stefano has a spring in his step. He still has a strong southern accent, and his lips are always fixed in a grin. He doesn't look people in the eye when he talks to them – not because he's shy but because he has no respect for them.

'Hey! I'm talking to you. Are you going to

turn round, you son of a bitch, or do I have to make you?'

Patrick stops. There is no escape – there never is.

He looks up at the boy for a second, then goes back to staring at the pavement.

Then someone else speaks: 'Hey, dickhead, you don't talk to my brother like that! Don't you know he does martial arts? Don't you know that the only reason he doesn't give you a good kicking is because he doesn't want to get suspended just because of a dickhead like you? So shut your mouth before any more shit comes out of it.'

The boy is frozen to the spot. The usual scenario, with him in charge, has been cut short. He looks round and realises that everyone is watching him as he gets it from this cow, blonde and slender, with ice-cold eyes and her sweatshirt hood pulled up over her head, she clenches her fists as she stands staring at him.

'Oh, so you're another one –'

Eva is suddenly standing just an inch away from him and his words come abruptly to a halt.

'You can say whatever you want about your own mother, but not ours,' she says, lifting her chin.

He doesn't know what to do. Eva snatches the stiff cardboard folder from his hands and says: 'Watch and learn.'

A crowd of students surrounds them. Eva moves closer to Patrick, and whispers: 'Just like in the training sessions.'

Then she says 'high kick' and holds up the folder.

For a moment Patrick doesn't move, but then,

swivelling from the pelvis, he kicks the target. She carries on, prompting him with 'low', 'middle', and he hits the folder each time with all the force he can muster. And for once his co-ordination is spot on. For once his kicks are direct and sharp. He's not ploughing a field, as the coach always jokes about him.

This morning Patrick feels that his legs are actually part of him. He's no longer stiff like a Playmobil figure, its legs remaining straight even when you try to make them sit down.

He is a champion now, with his legs are made of flesh and bone, not wood. He's not a puppet any more, and he kicks that fucking folder with all the strength that's inside him.

Soon the sheets of paper start to fly everywhere. The folder is totally destroyed, in tatters.

'I've told my brother not to worry if one of these days we get a letter from the headmaster to say he's been suspended. Anyway, I'm old enough to be the one who signs stuff for him. Today is the last time you ever speak to him. You hear what I'm saying? The last time.'

Then Eva takes Patrick by the arm and they walk off together, leaving Stefano surrounded by a cloud of laughter, trying to collect the sheets of paper that are fluttering down the street.

'I don't believe it. I did it! You made me do it. He was speechless!' Patrick says, incredulous.

'I didn't do anything. It was you that smashed that creep's folder. Just think now, if your mother knew you could defend yourself like that, she'd be so proud of you.'

Patrick believes that his mother has seen what he did, because from up there she is always watching him, though she never says anything. She just smiles.

CHAPTER 52

Marconi is in a bad mood today, and currently when he's in a bad mood, it's always got something to do with the Black Widow investigation.

The fact is that, over the last few days, so many of his ideas seem to have been proved right, and the profile of the murderer has started to materialise out of the fog of clues and hunches, even if the details still aren't totally clear.

That murder in the Carracci area has also recently been attributed to her. It was obviously her first time, because she had to strike the victim five times before killing him – a savage cut to the throat with a small yellow Stanley knife, which she left next to the body. Since then she has gradually refined her methods, becoming more skilful – and more lethal.

One decisive blow, by now she never gets her hands dirty. And the choice of weapon is never accidental. A sharp razor in the case of the lorry driver. No fingerprints. Some sort of antique sharpened specially for the occasion. Then the hairpin, used like a dagger.

She prepares her weapons in advance and goes into the city like a huntress.

Marconi doesn't agree with the profile drawn up by the psychologist: an extremely cold person; someone who has developed a feeling of hatred towards a father figure, and therefore towards all men. For him, she's not a woman who is indifferent, rather she's determined.

Determined to clean up the streets, as if that's an act of revenge.

She goes out armed and ready, but perhaps in her heart she hopes she won't meet anyone intent on doing evil. Yet she always does encounter someone, although her provocative way of dressing certainly helps.

The description from the waitress in the service station matches what they later told him at the nightclub: slightly over one metre sixty tall, blonde, red lips, light-coloured eyes and sexy clothes. A girl who definitely doesn't go unnoticed.

But since he talked to the weirdo selling the hairpins, everything seems to have gone back to square one. Marconi is annoyed, confused. He's virtually certain that the weapon was one of the guy's hairpins, that much is true. The vendor instantly recognised the gem as one of his.

'My jewels are like my children,' he had said. 'I could pick them out from a whole pile of others.'

But then he had added a few details about the girl which Marconi wasn't expecting. Marconi doesn't, however, have too much confidence in what he was told – the hippie seemed more interested in trying every possible angle to scrounge a drink from him –

but at the same time he can't get out of his mind the way the guy described her.

A girl of medium height, possibly blonde, with an anonymous face, but above all he claimed to remember her well because he had felt a violent dislike towards her.

'A spoilt little bitch. You know the type – looking like there's a nasty smell right under their nose. The sort who doesn't respect artists but buys things just 'cause they like owning things, collecting them – perhaps even wearing them once, if they feel like it, but never more than once.'

And in addition there's the information received about the pistol that fired the shots. The bullets extracted from the corpses lead him still further away from a solution: they turn everything upside down and bring him back to the starting point. A pistol, properly registered, that belongs to a rich entrepreneur from Bologna, a Signor Montanarini, esteemed member of the Rotary Club, collector of guns, personal friend of the *questore*.

He told them he hadn't even noticed that the pistol was missing. He keeps the guns in his study, some hanging on the walls, some arranged in cases and some locked up in drawers.

'I haven't cleaned them all for months, so it could have disappeared at any time,' he said. No sign of a burglary. 'Perhaps I'd forgotten to close the drawer, but at least the study door's always locked,' he explained to the *questore*. Yes, because it was the *questore* himself who insisted on asking the questions.

The entrepreneur added that he often holds parties

in his villa, but he rules out the possibility of one of his illustrious guests – who often include the *questore* and his wife – having stolen it. And then there's the video surveillance system, which captures every suspect movement, but for 'reasons of privacy' not a single tape has made it as far as the police station. None of the recordings that Marconi himself has seen is relates to the robbery in question.

No one knows, therefore, how the pistol disappeared, and, besides, Montanarini has already been inconvenienced enough.

'Please, nothing else,' Marconi blurts aloud. He's really angry about this obvious muddying of the waters.

He feels a bit like a stagnant puddle of water. The rain has stopped and he's just left there: he can't flow anywhere and soon he'll evaporate under the warmth of the sun. He will eventually disappear – without having been too much of a nuisance – just as the Black Widow is getting further away from him, and fading back into the fog again.

He would like to call Viola. He would like to see her sad smile again.

In the last few days all he's had time to do is interview the various witnesses again.

An old lady has joined the list of them. She explains that she hasn't been in touch before because her husband doesn't want any trouble, but, after having seen that programme on *Raidue*, about the killer in high heels, and then a bit of the press conference, she'd made up her mind to come in. She has sworn that, in Via de' Castagnoli, she saw – and it was definitely the evening of the murder – a pretty girl in a black raincoat, platinum blonde. She looked like Marilyn Monroe, she added.

'I was hot. I never usually open the window because of those horrible tramps who often sleep right under my flat, with their dogs. They're so dirty and rude. But that evening I decided to get a breath of air. My husband was asleep, when I opened the shutter and I saw her. She was walking along, in a hurry. I live in Via del Guasto, just round the corner from where they found that man. The dead man, I mean. I thought to myself: what is such a pretty girl doing out at this time of night?'

'Hello?'

'Don't you recognise my voice?'

A warm, enticing voice. A voice that ensnares you and won't let you rise back to the surface. Like quicksand.

'Who's speaking?'

'Have you forgotten me already?'

Marconi doesn't know what to say. The inviting voice on the other end of the line seems to reawaken his dull senses on this foggy Monday, in the middle of the afternoon.

'It's Samantha. A couple of days ago I saw the programme on –'

'"The killer in high heels",' Marconi interrupts her. He hates journalists, and fucking press conferences – and fuck Frolli too, who made up that name to grab the public's attention.

'I saw you, Inspector Marconi. What a little rascal you've been!'

'I couldn't –'

'I know, I know. But you're not very photogenic. Much better-looking in person.'

'How did you get my number?'

'Easy. I called the police station and told them I had important information on the Black Widow case to give personally to Inspector Marconi.'

Marconi doesn't respond to that. He doesn't know whether to tell her that what she did isn't ethical, but 'ethical' isn't a word he uses.

'You were so crafty, pretending to be a disappointed lover…'

'Nothing personal. I was undercover…'

'Don't worry. I understand. In fact I called you to help you out with your investigation.'

'You've remembered something?'

'No, nothing about your girlfriend.' She explodes in a brief, and startling, burst of laughter. 'But this weekend there's to be a very, very interesting party.'

'And what has the party got to do with the investigation?'

'It's a party that's been advertised everywhere on the underground scene. I can't get her out of my mind. If you really want to know the truth, I've still got her taste in my mouth.'

Marconi swallows. His saliva goes down like cement that's not quite set.

'Come with me to the party. That way you could win my forgiveness and at the same time, if you're lucky, you might also catch your killer. It's a fancy dress party. Aren't you going to ask me what the theme is?'

'You're going to tell me anyway, aren't you?'

"Marilyn Superstar is not dead". On the flyer it says that girls need to wear platinum-blonde wigs. Doesn't that remind you of anything?'

'Where do you live?'

CHAPTER 53

'Excuse me, Giulia. I need the bathroom. Do you mind?'

'Of course not – what a question! Use whichever one you want. You know where they are.'

The ringtone sounds, with the latest song by Biagio Antonacci.

'Hello. Oh, hi, Luca... No, I can't this evening. I've got my friend, Eva, here – you know, the girl who's a bit depressed. She hasn't got anyone and the fact is I feel sorry for her. I'm keeping her company... Yes, yes, we'll do it some other time... Bye. Love you.'

Giulia feels a sense of satisfaction in claiming Eva is depressed – it makes herself feel better – and she now pretends not to notice that her friend isn't depressed at all. On the contrary, Eva has never been in such good shape as she is at the moment.

At work she has become firmly entrenched in the creative team. She has had a raise, and she has bought a new car. And now it's Giulia who has to do the scanning for her friend. Eva looks radiant – damn her, and the day she made her join the gym.

'You've taken ages.'

'Sorry, but you know I always get lost in your stately home. Where's Giovanna today?'

'Giovanna?'

'The maid.'

'What are you on about? Why should you care where the maid is?'

'Sorry. I wanted to ask her if she'd make a swan for my sister. I'm going to dinner at my parents' tonight and I wanted to give it her as a present.'

'Today's Wednesday – it's her half day off. By the way, if anyone asks about me this evening, I'm with you, OK?'

'No problem: we're always together. Are you seeing Luca?'

'No, Fabrizio – someone I met last night, as I was doing Latin American dancing with Stefania. And if anyone phones you, I'm in the bathroom and my mobile needs recharging, so it's switched off in my bag.'

'OK, Giulia, but you know no one ever calls me.'

'It gets on my nerves that you're always so questioning. Is it too much to ask that you just say yes?'

'You're in a bad mood today. Is there something wrong? You've been a bit strange lately.'

'Nothing. Well... it's just that it's my birthday soon and I've asked my father for a special present, but he doesn't want to know and I don't know how to persuade him.'

'Insist. You're very good at getting men to change their minds.'

'Hmm... but he's been very nervy recently, my father, so I don't know. But how come you're telling me that I've changed... Just look at yourself! You're never around in the evening. I know you see your parents twice a week – at most – but when I ask you to have supper with me, you always come up with excuses. You haven't found a lover you don't want to tell me about, have you?' Giulia holds her breath.

'No, there's no lover... Anyway, you'd better get ready or Fabrizio will be annoyed. Let me do your hair. I'll put it in a plait – you always look good with your hair tied back. Am I being nosy if I ask you what you've asked for for your birthday that's so special?'

'Er... OK, I'll tell you. You'd soon see it anyway. I want a Cabriolet coupé. I adore them.'

Eva stops plaiting for a second. Then she starts again, moving her hands rapidly in and around Giulia's ash-blonde hair, while Giulia sits without talking and stares at her red, polished nails.

'Finished! Have a look.' Eva interrupts the silence.

'I look awful! I look like my grandmother.' And she starts to undo the just-plaited hair.

'I'm off now, Giulia. I need to spend a bit of time with Miew. Tonight I'm at my parents, so I'll be leaving her on her own again.'

'She's not a child... Oh, well, off you go. Of course, letting a cat run your life...'

'You know...'

'No. Go, go. It's just that I was hoping to talk to you for a bit.'

'But didn't you say you were in a hurry?'

'Yes, I am in a hurry, but not that much of a hurry.'

'What is it? Is it still about your father?'

'No.' Guilia's face clouds over and she rests her hands in her lap.

'What is it, Giuli?'

'No, go. Think of your cat. It doesn't matter.'

Eva starts for the door but then turns back.

Never look back, the special lady used to tell her when she was small.

Looking back means being weak.

Looking back means letting someone else run your life.

Eva doesn't want to, but she looks back.

'Come on, tell me. Don't worry about Miew. I can always call my parents up and say I'll be half an hour late.'

She sits on the bed and waits. In silence.

Giulia lets a smile of victory appear on her lips.

She too has just been lost in a faraway memory. A memory that smells of talcum powder.

Talcum powder. She used to love that pink crystal box. She loved to lift the lid carefully and let the sweet smell spread over her.

She would breathe gently, the lid in her hand.

Then she would put the box down on the blue tiles of the bathroom that was in her old house – her old place was enormous, but still a hovel compared with the villa she lives in now.

She would wait a few seconds more, and then would take up the powder-puff. It was a magical thing.

A white cloud.

She would start to stroke her rosy cheeks. She breathed in the perfume.

The perfume of a woman.

The perfume of desire.

One day her mother had called out for her. She heard her footsteps in the corridor, getting closer and closer.

In the midst of that soft, white intimacy, her mother's voice felt like a slap; she felt violated.

A sudden movement and... the white cloud that had been transporting her to faraway lands, the lands of dreams, of hidden desires, dropped into a whirlwind of powder.

White.

Then the fog had settled, slowly. As if time had stopped.

Silence.

The end of a dream.

A thousand pieces of crystal covered in a blanket. The blanket was as light as settled fog, and yet it seemed to her to weigh down heavily.

'I'm still here. I'm waiting. What did you want to tell me, Giulia?'

The girl turns. 'Nothing, really. I'll tell you another time. Don't worry, it doesn't matter.'

Eva waits for the bus in the half light of the city, which swallows her up. She thinks about how she really has changed: the sad, newborn infant inside her has become a woman, a woman who knows what she wants.

Her mobile phone rings.

CHAPTER 54

A block of flats. Like so many others looming behind the incessant stream of cars in Via Stalingrado.

Marconi looks up, out of the car window, and tries to count the floors.

The car door opens.

A leg as smooth as silk appears.

She gets in, along with her perfume.

A perfume that pushes the ordinary air out of its way.

She demands attention.

He stares at her, with his mouth half open, as if his eyes aren't enough to take in such a breathtaking vision.

She is demanding.

She is wearing a gold lurex outfit that wraps itself around her, embraces her. A slit on the left side reveals her black stockings. She is dressed, but it's as if she's wearing nothing. Pornographic.

A curly blonde wig clashes with her eyebrows, which are black as night.

She is beautiful. Gratuitously beautiful.

Beautiful in a way that fills both your consciousness and the space that surrounds her.

'Here I am. Have you been waiting long?'

'No, only about five minutes.'

'Let's go. I'll tell you the way.'

He starts the car and immediately she rests her hand on his as he holds the gearstick. Marconi moves his hand away, hurriedly, and for a moment doesn't know where to put it. Then he rests it on the steering wheel. When a car brakes in front of him, the gears don't engage. The car screeches.

'Sorry, but I need a bit of space when I'm driving,' he mumbles.

She fills the space.

Let's hope we get there soon.

I'm going to get a result this evening.

Thoughts. Thoughts that run into each other. Bouncing around within the car.

'Do you like your work?'

'Yes.'

'I would've liked to have been a police woman. Don't you think I'd be sexy in a miniskirt with a badge?'

'I've never had a female partner, but I don't think policewomen go around in miniskirts.'

'What have you got against miniskirts? There's no way you're a feminist?'

'I'm just saying they're impractical.'

'Minis *are* practical and, anyway, what would *you* know? Or do you like wearing women's clothes in your spare time?'

'What do you mean? I don't do that stuff. I was

just saying... Well, they don't seem practical to me. And then, working with so many men, it could cause embarrassment.'

'It wouldn't embarrass me at all – on the contrary. In fact I'd be doing a good deed by brightening up my colleagues' workdays, wouldn't you say?'

'Probably.'

'Probably, or definitely? There's a difference.'

'Definitely, definitely.'

'I could be wrong, but are you shy?'

'Me, shy? No, I've never been shy.'

'Ah, I see. You've never been shy.'

The gears shriek again.

Fuck. What's going on? I didn't even crunch the gears like this when I was learning to drive.

'So, it's not true that your girlfriend dumped you?'

'Well, no. I told you that just to get information.'

'For a cop as cute as you, I would've given you the information anyway. Or, of course, you could've squeezed it out of me. By force.'

Marconi turns on the radio.

She switches it off. 'I prefer talking.'

He starts to whistle softly.

'Left at the traffic lights. Have you lived in Bologna long?'

'A few years.'

'But are you always so mysterious? You never give anything away.'

'What about you?'

'Take the second turning at the roundabout. It's been a few years for me here as well. Turn right. We're here. Look for somewhere to park.'

'But you could've told me the party was here, at Salara.'

'What? So you could've just said "Let's meet there"?'

Marconi doesn't answer. It's true: he would have said that. It would have been his instinctive response.

'They're leaving. Park there.'

A boy in glasses – who must have got the wrong evening – is rushing away from the space with a girl. She's wearing glasses too.

'But isn't this a gay club? I once arranged to meet a colleague here by mistake, and I ended up having to explain myself to a sort of dwarf dressed… ambiguously.'

Samantha bursts out laughing.

'You're so narrow-minded! They have some great nights, so I often come here.'

'But does that mean you're…?'

'I'm me. And if you want to know if I like men as well, I can prove that to you now.' She crosses her legs, and thus uncovers even more of her thigh.

'Let's go.' Marconi opens the car door.

He's about to cross the road when he realises that she's not behind him.

The girl is eyeing him with a mischievous smile through the slightly steamed-up window. She waves at him to come and open her door.

Women. So keen to take the initiative, and yet they can't even open a car door by themselves.

He flings open the door clumsily. She holds out her hand and waits a second or two for him to notice it and take it in his. Then she gets out of the vehicle, leaning lightly against him.

They go in together. Marconi a step behind her.

211

'Do you have a pass?' demands a mannish-looking girl at the ticket desk.

'What?'

'You need a pass to get in,' she says, sounding pissed off.

'But I won't be coming again, so why would I want a pass?'

'You need a pass to get in tonight. If you don't come again, that's your business. I don't know... these straight shits who come here and think they can do whatever they like.'

'What?'

Samantha approaches the short-haired girl and gently touches her hand. She whispers something in her ear.

'OK, Sam, OK. But if were you I wouldn't go round with certain people. Do me a favour and take him away.'

'But what did you say to her?'

No answer. In the meantime, an irritated queue has been building up behind Marconi, who – who at one metre eighty-seven tall, and distinctly uneasy – is blocking the entrance.

Samantha grabs his arm. She is laughing, enjoying herself, not at all embarrassed. She likes impetuous men. As well as lots of other types of men – and women.

They head down a staircase with ancient, worn stone steps.

They go round in a sort of spiral. She clings on to the wrought-iron handrail. There are girls chatting on either side of the steps. They meet the first Marilyn, who looks more like a young Sandra Milo.

They get to the bottom of the stone stairs. There aren't many people there yet.

Two very young girls – two gothic dolls in tulle tutus and with boots laced up to the knee – are sitting on a bench talking to each other, one virtually pressing against the mouth of the other.

'But they're not lesbians, are they?'

'What?'

'Those girls over there, dressed like princesses. They can't be lesbians, can they?'

'Do you ever leave your house? God, you're such a yokel!'

'Me, a yokel?' Now it's him repeating the last word someone's spoken, and it sounds just as stupid as when other people do it to him.

'Are you going to get me a drink?'

'Of course.'

As he passes them, the policeman stares down at the two young girls. *Fuck, they can't be more than seventeen under all that black make-up.* They are holding hands, and teasing each other like a couple of lovers.

The women behind the bar all look like would-be lorry drivers. They don't look him in the eye when he orders two neat vodkas with a splash of lemon – the drink his companion has asked for. She, however, is already deep in conversation with one of the club's PR people.

Holding the two glasses, he watches her. The woman now with her behaves like a man: she gazes tenderly at Samantha's face, and her eyes – little bright buttons – sparkle with desire.

He starts drinking through one of the straws.

A group of fake blondes fills the space with vague chatter and garish colours. He watches them from behind. Carnival wigs, the plastic hair parted on one side and half covering their foreheads. Perhaps they bought them in bulk during a sale at some toy shop.

He gets the wrong straw this time and drinks from the second glass. The ice is starting to melt.

Samantha glances over at him while she flirts with her friend. Then she gives her a kiss on the mouth and comes over to Marconi.

'Here I am. Miss me?' She holds out her hand to take her drink. 'But they're both half empty.'

He blushes. She grins.

'So, what's the plan?' asks Marconi. 'I've come alone. Like you asked me to.'

'Oh, you sound like you're in some film, so I suppose I should, too. Let's see now. Stay close to me. When I spot the suspect, I'll try not to attract her attention. But you mustn't lose sight of your one and only witness.'

'But you're not really a –'

'Of course I am. A witness in danger. That's exciting, so don't say it's not true. Let me have some fun.' And she moves closer to him with an eager expression.

'Have your fun, then. *What can I tell you?*' It's a phrase he has adopted from Tommasi's repertoire.

And, speaking of Tommasi, he is still looking for a place to park in front of the club while two other policemen are waiting in a vehicle somewhere on the main road, expecting instructions.

It doesn't take long for the platinum wigs to take over the whole room. They're everywhere. Clones who are by degree more or less grotesque, more or less hairy.

There's even a Marilyn with a black moustache. 'God, he's repulsive,' the inspector grunts.

Samantha laughs. She really does find him entertaining.

'The music's starting. Let's have a wander round.'

A sort of turret erected inside the club lends it a certain atmosphere. Black curtains hang from the walls. Large oil paintings of naked girls, inside kitsch frames. A stall with two smiling youngsters – a boy and a girl not in fancy dress – has a folder full of badges on display.

Marconi moves closer to get a better look. The glittering badges include some with pictures from the cartoons he used to watch as a child. He starts to name them, out loud, pointing at each one in turn.

'Kotetsu Jeeg, the steel robot – I really liked him. Captain Harlock – that's amazing! And there's Sampei. Did you used to watch Sampei? How did the theme tune go?' And he starts to sing it. 'No, it's Tigerman! How much are they?'

'One Euro each,' the boy answers.

'Wow, that's cheap... Where do you find them? No, look! There's Carletto, Prince of Monsters... and Gigi la Trottola. I used to think it was so funny they way he went around stealing knickers...'

'Can you get out of the way? Other people would like to have a look.'

Another frustrated lorry driver. This is too much.

'Just wait your turn, like everyone else.' He has regressed to his childhood.

The girl pushes in and stands next to him. She hardly has time to point out Lady Oscar, a real lesbian icon, to her friend, before Marconi regains his spot.

'So, if I buy a few, will you give me a discount?'

'OK,' the girl says without hesitating. 'Five Euros for six.'

'Ah, but six won't be enough. There're loads of them I like... No! Films, too, I don't believe it! *Reservoir Dogs* – God, what a film! Igor from *Young Frankenstein*. I can't believe it...'

'You're not going to start listing all of them, are you? You're not the only one here. If you like, I can show that I recognise them all too – if you'll only let me.'

'Oh, why don't you go have a wander round while I'm looking through these. Leave me in peace while I choose what I want. So... I absolutely must have Gigi, Carletto, the robot Daitarn 3... No! It's Lupin!'

'Why don't you buy Fujiko for me? Don't you think I look like her?'

Marconi finally remembers that he's not come here on his own. 'Of course. Choose another one as well, if you like.'

'Look, it's Creamy and Bia. Did you used to watch Bia?' Samantha starts to sing the theme song, her wig swaying from side to side.

'Are you two ever going to get out of the way?'

'Just a minute.' Being a good policeman, Marconi is trying to keep things calm. 'One at a time. Take it easy.'

'Fuck taking it easy. You're the one's who's standing in the way.'

'That's because I was here first.'

The two people behind the stall look at each other, bewildered by what's now going on, and they smile as the boy tries to find Fujiko in a small, overflowing bag of badges.

'Bia as well. I have to have that one.'

'How many is that now?' Marconi asks.

'With Bia, it's six.'

'Let's get to ten at least.'

He bends over the stall, looking like a child confronting a jar of Nutella.

'It's her. God, it's her!'

'Her?'

'What do you mean "her"? I just saw her walking past us, the murderer.'

'Don't say "murderer". Are you mad?' Marconi covers her mouth with his hand. 'Put them on one side for me, and I'll come back and get them later,' he shouts as Samantha drags him away.

Behind them, a chorus exclaims in unison: 'At last!'

'Where? Where?'

'She was there.' Samantha indicates a vague area in the dark.

'Fuck, let's hope she's still there. It's chaos. Are you sure?'

'I *told* you, it was her.'

They walk round, trying to squeeze their way through the Marilyns – both male and female – and all the other people dressed in black.

'I can't see her any more.'

Fuck. I've missed out on those badges for nothing.

Marconi signals imperceptibly to Tommasi, who is standing to one side, leaning against a pillar.

217

'It's far too crowded, but at least we know she's here.'

'We need to be careful.'

'Let's have a look outside. Perhaps she's in the toilets – they have some chemical loos out front.'

'OK, it's worth a shot.'

They make for the exit.

'Come on, whip me!'

A middle-aged man, wearing make-up like a woman, a miniskirt hardly covering his arse and high-heeled shoes, hands a leather whip to a boy who is looking a bit scared. He doesn't know what to do with it. He holds it up, but only because it happens to be in his hand.

'You don't know how to do anything!' exclaims the man, grabbing the whip from the boy's hand. And, as if by magic, it ends up in Marconi's grasp. *As usual, here I am in the wrong place at the wrong time*, he thinks, finding himself with something in his hands that he has no intention of using on those flabby buttocks.

Samantha takes it away from him. She takes the whip quickly, as if they're playing that children's game where you pass the bomb and the child who has it when time's up incurs a forfeit. She, however, holds on to it tightly and starts to lash the older man.

'What the fuck are you doing?'

She doesn't answer but whips the man even harder. His skirt soon rides up and passers-by grimace with disgust. Marconi notices that one of his balls has just escaped from his too-tight thong and now hangs happily exposed, enjoying its new-found freedom.

This really is too much. Marconi heads for the toilets alone.

The men's loos are empty, but outside the ladies, there's a long queue.

A very pretty girl, natural blonde hair, red lips clasped round a cigarette, is trying to find her lighter inside her tiny bag.

He would like to be able to light the cigarette for her, but he doesn't smoke. So he turns to a stocky girl wearing make-up that makes her look like one of the living dead: 'Excuse me,' and uses his thumb and index finger to mime what he wants.

'Here you are.' She politely holds out her lighter.

Marconi runs back to the blonde and gives her a light without comment.

'Thanks. I couldn't find mine. My bag's too small... and too full.'

'No problem.'

'What a nice accent you have. You're not from around here.'

'Originally I'm from Modena. But I lived in France for a year, so that could be why. Do you have a pseudonym?' he adds.

What a fucking stupid question.

She looks at him, puzzled.

'I mean... it's just that everyone here seems to use made-up names. Shit, don't worry about it.'

'Oh, I didn't know what you meant. Yes, of course I have another name. You can express yourself better if you choose your own name, don't you think? I don't like those names that other people have given you. I'm Cassandra.'

'That's a really nice name.'

I'm such a piece of shit.

'And you? You don't have a name you use here, do you?'

'Of course I do! I'm... Renegade.'

'Renegade?!' Not again! She has done exactly what he himself did earlier: Marconi knows for certain that he's said something stupid, because she has repeated, as a question, what he has just said.

'Yes. Not great, is it?'

She can't hold back her giggling.

'Sorry.' The stocky girl is signaling that she wants her lighter back, mimicking the same gesture he used a second ago.

'That's mine,' she reminds him.

'Oh, sorry.' He roots around in his pocket and gives the lighter back to its owner, then turns his attention back to Cassandra.

She's beautiful when she laughs.

She covers her mouth with a slender hand. Red nail varnish, as red as her lipstick.

'The queue's too long here. If you want, I can keep a look-out and you can use the gents.'

'I don't know...'

'You're perfectly safe. I'm a...'

Shit. I almost told her. What a cretin! 'I'm a nice boy.'

'OK, then. I'll be quick. But, please, don't let anyone in.'

'OK. I'll go in with you and wait in the corridor.'

She locks herself in the cubicle. He hears a copious rush of urine.

She's now finished. The door opens and the girl

pauses on the threshold, for a moment. She seems to be smiling. Blonde, beautiful. For an instant Marconi thinks about how the lorry driver must have felt in that motorway toilet, just before he was died.

'Thanks.'

He goes out first and holds out his hand to help her down the three steps, which are almost too steep for the high heels she's wearing.

Samantha is watching them from a distance. 'Thank God, you were so shy with me, you bastard,' and she turns on her heels.

'Is that your girlfriend?'

He looks at her, speechless, then manages to mumble, 'I'm sorry', before running off in the same direction as Samantha's fleeing shadow.

CHAPTER 55

Life. It's strange, is life.

You can feel it throbbing inside you – it's yours – but anyone, or anything, at any moment, or any illness, can appear and take it away from you, just like that. *Steal* it from you.

Sometimes you live and nothing more; sometimes you think and live; sometimes you let life happen to you, and you waste it. Life.

The boy's face is contorted in a grimace of pain. Lying down. Or perhaps he's sitting. Sitting but looking like he's lying down, because he seems to have slid forward under the weight of his body that he can't support any more.

Life has flown out of him. Forever. It won't be coming back.

At this time of day, he should be in the square, showing off the double jump he has learned to do on his skateboard. But he can't do that any more. He has a wound, long and dark. The crack through which his life flew out of him.

He looks but he can't see. He is there, sitting, but looking like he's lying down. He seems to be waiting in the shade of a leafless tree, a tree lost in the darkness of a night that has witnessed so many things but can't tell a soul.

CHAPTER 56

'Hey, beautiful. Let me buy you a drink.'
'No.'
'You should loose that attitude. It's doesn't suit you, you know.'

She doesn't answer. Instead, she crosses her legs and flicks her hair to one side.

'Hey, I'm talking to you. Didn't you hear me?'

The girl gets up and heads towards the exit.

Shit, where has she gone. 'Get out of my way!'

What a cock-up, damn! And now what the fuck am I going to do?

The club is now full: zombie girls dressed in sequins and voile, unnaturally white skin and red lips. Platinum-blonde wigs that flutter round the room. It's like a nightmare. But he's awake.

This isn't his sort of place. The music is so loud that it makes him lose all sense of direction.

Too much perfume, too much darkness, then

sudden light as bright as flashbulbs, making him even more lost in a world that isn't his, a world in which he doesn't know how to navigate. He needs to see the reality of things. He moves perfectly easily on the streets, in real life. There he can understand things, smell the stench of crime, see the colours in people's stares, hear the noise of danger. But not here.

Here everything is false, filtered. Fakery upon fakery, perfume on top of perfume, mixed up with the acidic smell of drugs. Drugs that alter your mind, transform things, distort your perspective.

It's as if he is being shunted along by the arms of the people he bumps into. His vision is blurred. A hunted animal.

He keeps returning to the same spot. He can't spot the exit. He keeps finding himself here, in front of the same painting: the naked girl with a mermaid's tail. Her eyes make her look ill, and she points with her finger. 'Look' she seems to be saying to him out of the frenzy of flashing lights, but he doesn't see anything.

He has never liked discos. He didn't ever go to them, even when he felt he might have done. Now he's too old. He's out of breath, and his head... what the fuck is happening to his head?

He bangs into another moving obstacle.

He feels like a skittle in a bowling alley, where huge bowling balls in platinum wigs are trying to knock him over. It's not even as if he's worth many points, but that counts for nothing in the middle of all this chaos.

He leans against a pillar.

Opposite him, the girl with the mermaid's tail now seems to be pointing at him directly. She looks at him without pity; she judges him with those implacable eyes – cruel, ringed with black. Marconi lowers his gaze but his head feels like it's gripped in a spiral that is spinning him round.

Everything is turning, like a whirlpool. He thinks he's going to lose his balance. He looks up again. He doesn't know how he got there, but he's almost in the middle of the room now. The moving objects start to bump into him again. They move him whenever, and wherever, they want.

He feels like a puppet... No, he's a skittle, and you still don't get many points if you knock him over. Here's another ball in a wig about to run him down. But he senses someone holding on to him – a gentle touch, vaguely familiar, friendly, cool.

A girl has grabbed him by the wrist. She gently leads him away. She seems to know where to take him. She seems to know the way. She has a nice smell, a real smell, the perfume of delicate flowers. He can only see the back of her neck, pale, with curls resting on it like caresses.

He follows her without breathing. They seem to fly past the deformed monsters; they can't touch either of them now. He sees the exit.

He finds himself in the open air, staring at the sky. He can breathe again.

He is alone. He looks round but there is no one near him. Just a cloud of that indefinable perfume that lingers even here, under the vastness of the black, welcoming sky. He leans back against the wall behind him while he wipes away the sweat with his hand. He breathes in.

He doesn't remember anything after that. He thinks he sees Samantha, at a distance.

'Let's go. I'll drive,' is the last phrase he hears.

CHAPTER 57

The bloody blade has ceased calling her. It has had its fill, for now.

It won't torture her any more.

For a while.

It gets thirsty more often now than it used to. It is like a baby who grows up but doesn't stop craving his mother's milk. He wants it again and again. That hurts. It hurts because he gets stronger and stronger; he attaches himself greedily to the breast and sucks out the liquid he has become dependent on. As soon as his mother takes him in her arms, he smells the sweet odour and he can't resist. He starts to scream, and he screams until she attaches him to her breast and he can start to breathe again. The little teeth that are already pushing through the gums shred his mother's delicate skin, but she can't help wanting to satisfy the flesh of her own flesh. It's a need that burns inside her, sadism and masochism uniting in a dance of life. The pain hurts her flesh but it gratifies her spirit.

CHAPTER 58

Marconi opens his eyes. His head is still spinning but now he can focus. He's experiencing some sort of hallucination. He remembers a dark corridor. He remembers climbing up stairs on legs as heavy as lead. But nothing more.

There is a slight tingling on his lips. He opens and closes his mouth. He feels numb.

His eyes become accustomed to the dim, orange-coloured light. He focuses more clearly. He sees a bed with dark, glossy sheets – a sea of unpleasant memories. He sees a low bedside table and a lamp covered with a piece of red material through which filters a disconcerting light.

He moves his head from side to side, quickly. He wants to awaken his senses, but all he does is make himself feel dizzy. He feels like he's going to fall. Instinctively he tries to put out his hands, but they stay where they are, as if glued to the arms of the chair he's sitting in.

He looks down and understands why. He is bound

to the chairs by adhesive tape wrapped around his wrists, his skin bruised by its vice-like grip.

He kicks out, but his legs are held firm too. He isn't able to see them, buried as he is amid the black leather of a comfortable and unusual prison.

He doesn't understand. He doesn't remember.

Then he hears a voice. A sing-song voice. A monstrous lullaby that makes his body stiffen, and brings him completely and instantaneously to his senses.

A half-closed door opens, letting in a dazzling light. All he can see is the dark shape of the person to whom the voice belongs.

Then she closes the door behind her, and finally she appears before him.

She is still wearing the blonde wig, but she has even more make-up than before. She seems to be covered in a patina of heavy make-up that flattens her features and makes her look like an antique doll. Her appearance frightens him.

She looks like one of those dolls that his grandmother used to sit on her hand-made lace bedspread. They had staring eyes, outlined in black. Rosy lips through which you could see tiny gleaming teeth. The little neck was separated by a deep cut from the rest of the body, so that the head seemed merely balanced on top. It looked like it would fall off at any moment.

They wore ornate clothes, covered in lace and frills.

They used to terrify him. He would watch them secretly, checking to make sure that they didn't blink.

Deceitful creatures that just pretended to be unreal, inert. Instead they chose to sit there, motionless, but ready to come to life and attack him at the right moment.

Here she is, just as he imagined. The doll has come to life. She moves, she looks at him and laughs, showing her small gleaming teeth.

She comes towards him wearing nothing but a black lace slip that plays with the orange light, revealing and then covering the bare legs that move beneath the light fabric.

She has something shiny in her hand. A kitchen knife. It seems out of place.

'You've been naughty tonight.' She reveals the white pearls of her teeth again. 'Mummy's going to punish you.' She comes closer.

Frenzied shadows are projected on to the wall. It looks like a canvas that is being covered by a painter's wild brushstrokes. She waves the knife and laughs, but it sounds like she's crying.

She stops.

She looks grotesque, standing there in front of him with her legs apart. 'Am I beautiful?' she asks.

Marconi stares at her. She is a waking nightmare. 'Yes, you're beautiful.'

'Liar. I know what you're thinking.'

He's thinking that perhaps his mind isn't working properly. Perhaps he has just said 'You're a waking nightmare' out loud.

'Do you like me?'

This time he thinks first to make sure he gives the correct answer. 'Yes, I like you.'

'I drugged you. You're an idiot, policeman.'

Marconi shakes his head. For an instant he thinks

231

that perhaps Tommasi spotted him while he was following her, dragging his legs, clearly confused.

'You're stupid,' she says.

'What are you going to do?'

'I'm going to make you pay.'

'What have I done?'

'You made a mistake. And now I'm going to punish you.'

Marconi starts to tug at his arms and legs to release them, but he only manages to make the armchair move imperceptibly forward.

She bends over. She is that some doll, he's sure of it, his grandmother's doll. It has pretended to be good for all this time, and now...

'You're scared, aren't you?'

'What do you think?'

She moves the knife towards the sweaty face of the policeman. His sweat smells acidic, of drugs. She caresses him with the blade, but doesn't cut him. The sound made by his rough stubble against the metal excites her. 'You're sure of yourself – because you're a man. But I'm in charge now.' And she holds her face close to his, as if she wants to inhale the life out of him.

'I'm scared. You're in charge. That OK?'

'Not yet.'

She stands up again, raises one leg, then rests it on his knee. He just has time to focus on what's happening, before he feels a razor-sharp pain. She raises and lowers her leg as is she's trying to kick him away and she drives her stiletto heel first into his thigh, now into his knee cap.

'What the fuck!'

'It hurts, doesn't it?'

'Stop it. You'll be in big trouble.' He tries to sound like that policeman in a film, but he can't remember which film.

She lifts her leg. She holds it raised for an instant, then kicks hard, the kick ending at his thigh. He clenches his teeth so as not to scream.

'I adore high heels.' And she leans over him again.

'What do you want from me?'

'I want you to want me as much as I want you. Do you want me?'

'Yes. Yes...'

'Liar. You're all the same, you men. Liars.' She is shouting now. 'Liars. Liars, phonies, bastards, pigs.'

Marconi really is scared. He is utterly alert, as if eager to enjoy this macabre spectacle in which he is the protagonist, defenceless, with his hands tied.

She raises the knife and brings it down level, with his stomach.

He closes his eyes, tightly. He doesn't want to see, just like when he was small and for a moment he was sure that the horrendous doll had moved, and when he preferred to close himself inside the darkness that he could create whenever he wanted. Perhaps, that way, the doll might have believed that her secret was safe and she would have spared him. At least for a while.

She is slashing his trousers. The fabric hisses under the blade, as it is guided by hysterical hands.

'You're all pigs. You make me mad. What should I do with you?' She seems to be raving now.

She carries on slicing, and screaming filth.

He feels shaken. The doll, with her eyes circled in black, is on her knees at his feet. And he has an erection.

CHAPTER 59

'Congratulations on that work you did for the shopping centre. I like it. It's snappy, lively, really dynamic advertising. Great, really great. But I... Eva, are you listening to me?' Mariangela asks.

'Yes, sorry. I'm not feeling too well today. I've got an awful headache.'

'Are you coming for a drink with us after work?'

'I can't. I've always got loads of things to do on Wednesdays.'

'OK, I won't try to persuade you. But go and get yourself a coffee – you need one. And ask Bruno to come to my office as you go out.'

Bruno is new. He has replaced Roberto – and not just at his desk.

'Giuli, do you want to come? Time for a coffee break.'

'I can't, any more. Always the same stuff – I'm sick of that scanner. I even dream about it at night!'

'Come on. Tomorrow's your birthday! You should

be happy. And what about your father? Did you follow my advice?'

'Yes. I'm meeting him today, like you suggested. Away from home and also away from where he works, so he doesn't get any distractions. We're meeting at his club, nice and relaxing, and –'

'And he'll say yes. I'm certain.'

'Let's hope so! At any rate, you're craftier than I thought.'

'Thank you. It's nice of you to say so, but I'm not sure I should take it as a compliment. Anyway, this evening I'm expecting you at mine. Miew and I have prepared a little supper for you, to thank you for everything you've done for us recently. And then you'll be able to tell me if you've persuaded him to buy you your new car.'

Giulia seems embarrassed, which is rare for her. 'I wasn't expecting you to do anything,' she says. 'And I thought I was being a bit annoying – about the car I mean.'

'Of course not, why should it annoy me? So I'll see you this evening. It'll be an unforgettable evening, I promise.'

Eva goes back to her desk. She is preparing a publicity campaign for a new type of urban vehicle. Ideas whirr around in her head. She thinks about the size of the car – easy to park, even in the smallest spaces. She wants to get across the idea of it making the most of every possibility, of grabbing every opportunity as it occurs, of a philosophy you can apply to every aspect of your life and to all of the decisions you make every day. 'The person who can make the most of every second chooses a car that doesn't loose a single moment,' she says out loud. Her gaze rests on the one red rose that stands out from the desk strewn with paperwork.

CHAPTER 60

The sun is high in the sky. The staring eyes are still searching upwards for something they can't see.

It will never again be dawn, never sunset.

The body was found an hour before. He seems astonished to be there, with all those people now buzzing around him. Around him, who has only ever had a small group of friends. His street friends will never again watch him doing his double jump on his skateboard.

'Where's Inspector Marconi?'

'He hasn't been answering his mobile since last night. I'm really worried. We were following…'

'Some women. So what's there to worry about?' Frolli sniggers.

There's another corpse, lying motionless, his eyes fixed on some undefined object.

Marconi has just woken up on the bed with black sheets, in a sea of unpleasant memories. He stares at something but he can't focus on it. He hurts all over. But he's alive.

He is naked. His face is contorted.

She opens eyes smudged with mascara. The smeared make-up makes it look like she is grieving. She looks like the sinner in some dreary painting, crying and pleading for forgiveness, overwhelmed and petrified by a dull pain, petrified.

Her lipstick has rubbed off. Her black hair hangs down limply on to breasts hidden by this funereal shroud.

Her wig lies on the floor, along with her slip.

She looks at him and smiles for a second.

He gets up without saying anything. He remembers he hasn't got any clothes on. Shreds of fabric he's abandoned, by the leather armchair, like strange confetti at the end of some grotesque carnival.

'I don't suppose you've got anything in my size.'

'I have. I've still got some of my ex's clothes, if that's OK. He was just a bit shorter than you.'

She gets up. In daylight she isn't frightening. Her voice has a vague, indefinable inflection; it's not a hellish singsong any more. She is a real woman, now. And she's got a great arse.

She opens a drawer and, leaning over it, rummages through a muddle of clothes, leather collars, and studded objects. Marconi spots a purple dildo and is grateful that she didn't use it on him last night.

'You're sick,' he says quietly.

'I know,' And without looking at him she throws him something black. A T-shirt with a skull, and HATE written in gothic letters. Then she hands him a pair of leather trousers.

'Underwear?'

'He never wore any.' Her voice hides a trace of sadness.

'Lovely. I hope at least you washed these occasionally.'

She comes towards him.

'Stay away from me.'

'Does that mean you didn't enjoy it?'

'Where's my mobile? My car keys?'

'Everything's in the car. Your keys are in the kitchen, on the table.'

The skin round his wrists and ankles stings a bit, and looks bruised. He had never done it before, while tied up.

'Oh well...' It's the last thing he says as he leaves the flat. Before he closes the door behind him, he sees a stuffed owl staring down at him from a shelf, with large, round glass eyes.

CHAPTER 61

Sitting on the floor, red hair covering her face, hands shaking. She would like to escape from her body, but her body ensnares her, weighs her down, doesn't let her stop existing. She is trembling.

She's in a prison constructed of images she wishes she could forget. Of words she wishes she had never heard.

Dreams and reality have become a single entity. She is tired of breathing. Tired of the screaming of her soul. She is silent. She would like to shout but instead she cries. It's the only thing she knows how to do.

CHAPTER 62

Where the fuck is my phone? And just at that moment it starts ringing.

Perfect timing.

Marconi answers. He feels that the day hasn't started as badly as it could have done. He's alive, the sun is shining, and no one has broken into the car to steal his mobile.

'Where the fuck have you been?'

'I had a few problems.'

'While you were out enjoying yourself at your fancy-dress night, and roping in – without permission – a police car and a plain-clothes detective, a minor's had his throat cut in the Montagnola park.'

'What?'

'Don't worry. They made me come back on duty this morning, after they found him. Since you weren't around…'

'I'll be there straight away.'

'Get a move on… you jerk,' yells Frolli. 'This isn't the end of it – the *questore* is furious. A friend of his, at the Roses Club –'

'But didn't you say it was a boy?'

'Keep up. No one gives a fuck about the boy. I'll see you at the club. They've killed someone important this time. Move your arse.' He slams down the receiver.

The traffic in Via Stalingrado is bumper to bumper. Marconi doesn't have time for this delay. He spots the pavement on his left and reverses the car, ending up with his bonnet sticking out into the oncoming traffic, causing a bedlam of near misses and dented bumbers, amid a deluge of blaring horns that precipitates all around him.

He joins in the chorus and starts to lean on his own horn. He holds up his arms, but the drivers in the other lane won't let him in and the queue of cars behind him is getting longer. He reaches down to find the siren. *Fuck,* he hid it in the boot the night before.

As he tries to move forward, a Mercedes barely avoids crashing into his bonnet.

The man behind him gets out of his car. He's a large and imposing man – not a very reassuring sight.

Marconi takes advantage of a red Fiat Uno with a woman driver, and he cuts straight across her path. Now the horns sound like they're screaming in unison at the cretin left standing in the middle of the road.

Marconi summons the nerve to shout 'Dickhead!' as he drives away, mentally working out an alternative route to the club.

CHAPTER 63

The smell of blood poisons the air before he even crosses the threshold. It permeates the walls, it insinuating itself into everything. It's like a punch to the stomach.

Marconi shows his badge to the security guard in the corridor, who's keeping onlookers and photographers at a distance while looking rather puzzled.

Tommasi notices Marconi and hastens towards him. 'Where have you been? It's been just one thing after another...' He looks Marconi up and down, bemused.

'I'll explain later. The *questore*?'

'He's just gone. He wanted to be the one to break the news to the victim's wife and daughter. He's furious, too. He's threatening to put us all back on the beat if we don't find the killer straight away.'

'Let's see.'

'In here. It's a mess, a fucking mess.'

Tommasi shows him the way. The sun filtering through the large window and shines like a spotlight on the corpse on the floor. He is lying on his back, legs wide open and at an angle, making him look like he's swimming in a sea of blood. The dead man is wearing an elegant grey Armani suit, and an expression of terror.

His eyes are wide open, and his torso and hands have been slashed repeatedly with a sharp weapon. An extremely deep wound to his throat, black as night, completes the macabre image.

Marconi momentarily feels that he is being swallowed up in a spiral of darkness. He sees himself tied to that armchair. He can picture the red light of the room, and the mad doll who played with him for what seemed like an eternity. He has fooled himself that the sun will have cancelled out everything. Like waking up from a nightmare. But it isn't like that. The vision of death follows him. It won't leave him in peace.

Tommasi interrupts the unnatural silence hovering in the room. 'A waiter found him about an hour ago. I've already taken his statement. The victim's Montanarini, the entrepreneur. That collector – the one same who had his antique pistol stolen.'

'Oh fuck.'

'I don't think everyone heard that.' The voice of Frolli behind him.

Marconi doesn't even turn round.

'An honorary member of the club, and one of its main backers,' Tommasi continues. 'He used to come here three times a week to play squash, have a sauna, business meetings – among other things. The waiter told me that this private room – there's a very long corridor from the main part of the building, so it's nice and remote – is often used by club members for trysts... if you know what I mean. The victim had told the waiters that he didn't want to be disturbed. They left a chilled bottle of champagne and two glasses, as they always do. By the way, the bottle's disappeared. Perhaps the killer wanted to celebrate.'

'That all?' Marconi asks.

'First his gun disappears, and it kills two pushers,' Follo interjects. 'And now he gets himself killed. This case stinks – almost as much as you do, Inspector. And what the fuck are you wearing?' Frolli says, holding up his hands and looking like he's about to start pulling his hair out.

Marconi looks down at himself. He has totally forgotten that he's dressed like some crazed fan of a heavy metal group.

'I was undercover.'

'Which means you haven't been home yet, eh?'

'Enough, OK? I'm really not in the mood.'

'Ah, he's not in the mood. Neither was I, first thing this morning, when they called me back on duty after only a few hours off.'

'I was following up an important lead.'

'Yes, I can see how good a lead it was. Two dead in the space of a few hours and you're nowhere to be found. Fantastic.'

'Listen...' Marconi begins.

'Careful what you say.'

'Look at this.' Galliera beckons them over.

He points at the long knife that has been placed

next to the victim, with three roses arranged on either side.

'It looks like a kitchen knife. The sort you use to cut meat.'

'It's not as if we'll find any fingerprints,' says Marconi, staring at the roses bathed in blood. It looks like a painting, of exceptional beauty and ferocity. Then his gaze falls on to the man's white shirt, stained with blood around chest height.

'Just a minute,' he says. 'Hey, you with the gloves, lift this up.' He is pointing at the dead man's jacket.

He observes for a moment and then says: 'These aren't splashes. They're fingerprints. They look like they come from bloodstained fingers. Here as well – on the inside pocket of the jacket.'

'The murderer was looking for something,' Tommasi exclaims.

Yes, and I'd give anything to know what.

As soon as he leaves the murder scene, Marconi rushes outside. He needs to see the sky. He needs to breathe.

CHAPTER 64

Eva is laying the table ready for her friend. She has bought everything she needs. Little pink candles and a larger one with a red heart to put in the centre of the cake. A cake made with cream and chocolate and decorated with strawberries.

She's also got some appetisers, but she didn't get them from Lina, where she bought the cake, even though she knows that theirs are really good. She preferred to order them from that bar near the Two Towers, so she could see the barman again. The one who was so nice. And so cute.

It was he himself who answered the phone, and Eva explained that she was the girl who had celebrated her birthday there a while ago.

'I remember you.'

She didn't believe him, but then he added: 'Who could ever forget eyes like yours?'

After work she had hurried over to pick up the appetisers, already ordered, and he had offered her a drink. A fruit-based cocktail, thirst-quenching. He had asked her where she usually hung out.

'I don't go out much. I don't know that many people here.'

The barman had handed her a card. On it was written his phone number with a smiley face drawn instead of a zero.

Miew is rubbing herself against Eva's legs. *Come on you, I'll have to wash my hands again.* The cat looks up at her, still wanting to be petted. *Oh, OK, then.* She bends down and takes Miew up in her arms. *You're the only one for me, do you know that? The one love of my life.* And she kisses her on the nose. The cat looks at her with large, luminous green eyes. 'And you're mine,' she seems to be saying, instead of a miaow.

CHAPTER 65

Marconi never usually goes home at lunchtime, but today isn't a usual day.

First, he absolutely must change his clothes.

Second, he feels dirty. Perhaps he really does smell, like that bastard Frolli suggested, given that he'd been sweating so much because of the drugs that crazy woman put in his drink. And perhaps also because of the fear he had felt.

More than anything he feels dirty, as if he has been violated deep inside. He thinks that perhaps he can now understand how women feel after they have been the victims of sexual violence. He tries to drive the idea from his head, as it hurts too much to think about it now. A nice shower is what he needs. But first an aspirin. He hates pills, but this time he really needs to take something, because every part of him hurts.

Both his body and his head.

He lets the steaming hot water flow over him. He scrubs with the soap where large purple bruises have appeared. On his wrists, his ankles, then the bite marks on his chest and neck, and the fingernail scratches on his back. He can't reach the scratches but he can feel them sting under the hot water.

While the water courses over his skin, scarlet images appear before his eyes, like the frames of a film. Of last night, of that narrow room, the claustrophobic space where he was imprisoned and where he had been thinking: *This is how it feels before you die.*

And, instead of him, other people had died, carried away by that unknown assassin on her black horse of death.

She has killed an old man and a boy, like in that song he used to sing when he was small.

He turns off the tap with a flick of his wrist and just stands there dripping and staring at the bright blue tiles. Then he reaches outside the white shower curtain, grabs the bathrobe that's always there – one fixed point in his too erratic life – and puts it on.

He drags himself to the armchair and sits down, his back to the room and his face turned towards the sun streaming through the blinds, puncturing the darkness of the room with tiny golden spirals.

He has too much to think about. So he tries not to think about anything.

He picks up his mobile to check the calls he missed during last night's bad dream.

He's never had so many phone calls. Thirty calls he hasn't answered.

Five from Tommasi, two from the police station, two from the *questore* (which doesn't bode well), three from Frolli, three numbers he doesn't recognise and five calls from Viola. He gives a start: he doesn't know why, but he's afraid for her. He is about to click on her name, but the phone starts ringing. The call is from a an unknown number.

The city is hidden under a blue veil. The sun has already set and darkness is resuming its territory.

He can't believe it. Everything is happening at once. One phone call after another.

As if everyone's conscience has been awakened at the same time.

As if fear has opened a Pandora's box of secrets.

Two telephone calls. Two women. Two truths that lay hidden but are now exposed to the light of day.

CHAPTER 66

E va sings happy birthday to Giulia, as she lights the candles.

The small, square table is set for two, with a checked green linen tablecloth.

Eva sings and watches her friend, who seems genuinely happy for once.

The tray that held the appetisers is empty. The last one is lying in Miew's bowl, the cat studying it, trying to work out how to eat it. In the meantime, the cake lends colour to the table and lights up the girls' greedy eyes.

'Thank you. Truly. No one has ever made a birthday tea for me like this. I mean... just for me, from the heart. And not just because it's expected.'

'Don't mention it. You've done so much for me over the last year, and I don't think I've ever thanked you properly.'

'Rubbish! I've not done anything, and that's the truth.'

'It's *not* true, Giulia. You've done so much for me.' And she clasps her friend's hand.

'You know, you're making me feel like a hypocrite...'

'Oh, stop it. Come on, you have to cut the cake.'

'Just a minute. Let me finish...'

'If that's what you want.'

'I've never done anything for anybody. I pretend to, perhaps, but really I only help other people if there's something in it for me. I'm not a nice person. But it's not my fault. I'm just like that. I've been like that for as long as I remember.'

'But you really have helped me a lot.'

'But only because I needed you. The truth is I'm lonely; I've got no one. Everything around me is all fake. You're the only real thing that's happened to me... and now I'm so embarrassed.' She looks down at the floor. Perhaps she's about to cry.

'Giulia, you saved my life, believe me,' and Eva squeezes her hand even tighter.

'You're so good to me, even about the car...'

'You shouldn't be embarrassed – quite the opposite. Tell me how it went.'

'He said yes, he's going to buy me it. He was as meek as a lamb. He must have been thinking about something else. I can't wait, I wanted it so much. Thanks for your advice – your idea was great.'

'I'm happy for you.'

'Really?'

'Yes, I told you.'

'Look what I stole for us from the club.' Giulia gets up and opens her orange Prada bag. 'Voilà, champagne for the girls!'

'Wow. I've never had champagne. Let's get rid of this cheap stuff first. There!' Eva throws back her head, and the contents of her glass disappear.

Giulia does the same. She grins. 'Cake first, or champagne?'

Miew seems more restless than usual. She jumps on to the sofa and miaows to attract attention.

'What's wrong with your cat today? She's insufferable.'

'Perhaps it's the moon.'

'What do you mean, "the moon"?' Giulia doesn't understand.

'Champagne?'

'OK, you ready?' And she shakes the bottle.

'We'll be soaked if you do that.'

Pop.

The champagne explodes in a roar of bubbles. The cat dives under the sofa.

The intercom buzzes.

Silence.

'Are you expecting someone?' Giulia asks, amazed.

'No. Perhaps they've pressed the wrong button. It happens all the time. They ring any bell to get someone to open the door. A real Casanova lives above me.'

'Just when we were about to have our toast.'

Eva pushes the button to open the door, and comes back to her chair.

'But what if it was for you?'

'It's never for me. I keep telling you, nobody ever wants me.'

Giulia stands still, with the two overflowing glasses

in her hands. She looks uncertain. She stares at the bubbles that swim to the surface and explode as they make contact with the air. She hands one glass to Eva. 'To us, and to friendship.' She raises her glass.

They can hear footsteps running up the stairs. The girls remain silent, as if there's an unspoken agreement between them to wait for something that's about to happen. Giulia clinks her glass against her friend's, a way of carrying on with her birthday. Her lips reach out to the golden liquid in a kiss that isn't consummated.

Someone bangs violently on the door, sounding like they might want to break it down. A voice shouts: 'Police! Open the door. We've got a search warrant.'

Eva jumps up, then freezes to the spot, while Giulia, panicking, starts to scream.

Seconds pass that seem to last for hours.

'Open up!'

The girl goes towards the door, one step at a time. She stops in front of the one defence she has left, before sliding back the bolt. Then she lowers the handle of the reinforced door. Stuck on the back of the door is a picture of her sister, aged five, wearing the salopettes from Candy Candy she used to own.

She steps back. Three men burst into the room.

One shows her his badge. 'Inspector Marconi,' he says, gazing into the girl's ice-cold eyes. She stares at him but doesn't say a word.

The other policemen are both holding guns. They look at the two girls. Marconi stares at Eva. He's sure he recognises her, and she too loses herself in his stare, silently, as she clenches her fists.

The light from the candles dance over the whipped cream, like restless ghosts on a windy night.

Marconi takes another step forward. He grabs Eva's arm and moves her out of the way.

'Giulia Montanarini, I'm arresting you for murder. For the murder of Enzo Montanarini, and others.'

'My father... dead? No... no!' cries Giulia, stepping backwards, her eyes full of tears. 'I haven't killed anyone!' she shouts hysterically. 'Help me, Eva. Help me! I haven't killed anyone.'

Eva flattens herself against the wall, to allow the other policemen past her. They move towards Giulia, who is now standing with her back to the window.

'No! Daddy! No!' And she lets herself fall to the floor.

The policemen lift her up bodily, the handcuffs close round her slender wrists. The wax from the candles on the cake drip like tears on to the blood-red strawberries.

'Congratulations, Inspector. You've solved the case less than six hours after the murder. And who would have thought it – Giulia? I've known her since she was just a child.' The *questore* shakes his hand. 'But tell me, Inspector, how did you do it?'

'I didn't do anything.' Marconi doesn't say it out of modesty, because he really hasn't done anything. 'I've got to go now,' he adds. 'My shift isn't over yet.'

CHAPTER 67

The doorbell rings, and yet again he's about to become the bearer of bad news.

Another closed door that's about to open. The pallid girl flings it open without even looking at him. She has been waiting for him, wide awake, for twenty-four hours – but the man who enters the semi-darkness of the too empty, too cold house isn't who she was expecting.

'Oh, it's you.'

'Viola, I have to talk to you.'

'I can't now. My boyfriend's due back and I don't want him to find you here.'

'Viola, sit down. I have to tell you something important.'

'Not now... please.' It seems to be a struggle for her to talk. She hides herself among the cushions on the sofa.

'It's about Marco.'

'What do you have to tell me about Marco? Something's happened to him, hasn't it?' She gets up and almost instantaneously is standing opposite him, her eyes shining, already moistening with tears.

'Take it easy, Viola. Come and sit down.' He likes to use her name. Viola. It sounds nice – delicate, soft.

'I don't want to sit down. I want to know what you came here to tell me, and then you must go.'

'I don't know how to tell you.'

She hangs on his every word, waiting, voraciously, leaning towards him.

She thinks about the roses in the blood. Yet that dream no longer interrupts her sleep. No longer calls to her. But that dream used to accompany the angel of death; she's certain of that.

'What's happened? What is it? Come on, tell me, you bastard!' She starts to beat her fists against his chest. The vampire bites still hurt, so Marconi grabs her slender arms and holds them still in a grasp that manages to be both determined and delicate.

But the girl cries out with pain, as if needles were hidden in that gentle touch. He lets go immediately, and sees them.

'God, what have you done...?'

'Keep away from me. Just tell me what you came for.'

Purple streaks across her white flesh. Cries tattooed on to the skin. They don't want to stay hidden any more.

She moves away from him.

'Marco's been arrested.'

For a second Viola seems relieved. The police officer isn't saying 'He's dead' like that earlier time she still remembers so well. But then she starts crying again. 'What has he done?' She stares out at the emptiness that surrounds her.

Marconi would like to tell her how Marco sold drugs to children, that he fucked several Romanian girls in exchange for drugs, and that he has killed a minor, without showing an ounce of pity.

He would also like to tell her that the girl who was keeping him hidden in her home grassed him up after he had given her a beating. Yes, Marco had made a big mistake there. He had thought he could treat some untamed girl like he treated his fiancée. But a girl like that doesn't like being controlled – even Marconi had realised that when he visited her regarding Mario Rossi, the man with the name used in the advert.

Marco had threatened her, hit her and, to frighten her, had even described to her how traitors like Fabietto ended up.

'I'm not asking much of you – just let me stay here a few days till things quieten down,' he had said to her, while still dirty. Still covered in blood and filth.

She had let him do whatever he wanted. Everything he wanted. She had even let him touch her with those hands stained with blood.

But then, the day after, after preparing a plate of spaghetti for him, after having smiled at him as she gazed into his eyes, she had gone out to buy some beer. And then she had called that number, the one written on the crumpled card that the cop had left her after the death of the man she had been living with, Mario Rossi.

But instead of all that, Marconi says, 'Drugs.'

'And that's why he didn't come home to me?'

'I imagine so.'

The rolled-up sleeves of her jumper, rumpled like the pain showing in every feature of her face, leave the still raw scars uncovered. They are of different lengths, different colours. The darkest must be the oldest; the ones that look red perhaps still smell of blood, the same smell that perfumes Marconi's own aching body.

He would like to hug her tight, but he doesn't move.

He looks at her head among the cushions, shaking with her deep sobbing. She is so fragile.

'And the roses?' She asks, still worried.

Marconi immediately understands what she is talking about. *The roses.*

He thinks about how the case has been solved without him even realising it.

The phone call to the police station from that woman with a strange accent, slightly forced, who said she was called Jin Holin and that she was the maid at the Montanarini house.

She had told them that she had found a gun hidden under the mattress of the daughter, Giulia, while she was making her bed that morning. She had then begged them not to involve her any further – she didn't want to risk losing her job.

Then they had gone to Montanarini's house. The wife was there on her own, devastated by the news of her husband's death. It was the maid's day off, like every Wednesday.

Signora Montanarini, answering in one syllable

like an automaton, without thinking, and without seeming aware of anything going on around her, had shown them to her daughter's room.

The gun was there. Hidden under the mattress. And that wasn't all. In the wardrobe, a dress in an oriental style, just like the one Samantha had described to him.

In the drawer of the dressing table, a huge bunch of keys and a metal hairpin missing one of its red jewels.

The jewel that was found in that cul-de-sac, behind the disco.

A puzzle put together far too easily. A puzzle where you can see how a piece will fit perfectly before you even try it.

And he doesn't swallow it. It doesn't add up. It's all too unexpected. All too perfect.

And perfection is only an illusion. He can't remember where he heard that, but he's convinced it really is true.

Before he sits down next to Viola, he picks up a threadbare, old teddy bear, lying abandoned on the armchair, and he rests it on her legs.

'I can't be on my own.'

'You aren't on your own.' He caresses her with his voice.

'The roses were covered in blood.'

Now he gently strokes her hair and he pictures the roses again. He pictures Giulia's face. He definitely hadn't imagined that she would look like that, his Black Widow.

'Giulia? We weren't very good parents,' her mother had confessed, standing in the middle of the room, holding a photograph of her daughter. 'She was a liar. She has always been a liar. She always wanted things... she wanted to have everything.'

'Signora Montanarini, come with me. Let's go downstairs. Perhaps you should call a doctor. Have you taken anything yet?'

'Yes, I had two of my tablets, but they aren't doing any good. They don't even make me sleep any more. She wanted a car. She wanted a convertible just like one of her friends got. She always wanted *everything*. She'd been begging her father for weeks. Her friend had been given a raise and bought the car, so Giulia had to have one too. She wanted that car so much... but to do this...'

She then burst into tears. On the sofa, she clasped the photo of her daughter, who now seemed to be sneering at her with that fake smile and all those white teeth surrounded by a bow of too-pink lipstick.

'Don't cry. It's all over.'

But Marconi isn't so sure of that.

He looks at the moon. It's red, unreal, magnetic. Perhaps it's the moon that controls women. The girl finally seems calm. She has fallen asleep.

Eva is staring at the moon as well. She stares at it, inhaling the light it gives off. She sees its reappearance, after such a long time, as a sign. She hugs Miew and thinks that a circle has been completed. She remembers the first time she did it, to that boy with a red scarf who wanted her money and had threatened her with an old yellow Stanley knife.

She had kicked him, hard. As hard as she could. She had heard a dull thud, and he had sunk on to his knees, his leg broken. He had tried to get up, and then she had struck him again in the face, without hesitating. A kick so forceful that she had shut him up for ever. Then, instinctively, she had picked up the knife from next to his body and had put it in her pocket, almost like a war trophy.

From that day on, she hasn't been able to stop. She does it for herself; she does it just to live. She needs to spill blood in order to cleanse herself... to clean up the world.

As if every drop spilt fills the emptiness she feels inside her. As if it can silence her fear, her anger.

She loves to tell herself that she does it for all of womankind. For her sister, for the girl sitting next to her on the bus, and for the girl going home now in the dark – although tonight the darkness pierced by the moonlight.

Sometimes someone has to be sacrificed for the greater good. Giulia's face, glowing in the light of the coloured candles, appears before her, but almost immediately Eva turns away from it.

And this time she doesn't turn back. Just like the special lady taught her.

On the table there's a small rectangular parcel, still wrapped up. Eva sits down, pours herself a glass of champagne, and unwraps it carefully. A red lipstick, as red as fire.

As red as blood.

She gets up and leaves the room to stand in front of the mirror in the corridor. She glides the colour over her lips.

She smiles.

Then she goes back into the kitchen and picks up the cat's bowl. She turns it over.

Stuck to the bottom with Sellotape is a small black cassette labelled 'CCTV – Montanarini villa – study', followed by a date... the day that Eva stole the pistol.

She pulls it loose and says to the cat: 'Tonight, Miew, we'll watch a very special film.'